BEHOLD, THE NEW HAS COME

Behold, The New Has Come

ARCADIAN BARRETT

Crow House Press

Copyright © 2022 by Arcadian Barrett

All rights reserved. No part of this book may be reproduced in any manner whatsoever without written permission except in the case of brief quotations embodied in critical articles and reviews.

Paperback: 978-1-7373795-3-9
Ebook: 978-1-7373795-4-6

Crow House Press
First Printing, 2022

CONTENTS

DEDICATION - vii

~ I ~
BEHOLD, THE NEW HAS COME
1

~ II ~
be renewed in the spirit of your mind
3

~ III ~
to the depths of the pit
12

~ IV ~
the old things have passed away
23

~ V ~
in you i take refuge
30

~ VI ~

bad company ruins good morals

42

~ VII ~

offer your bodies as a living sacrifice

54

~ VIII ~

let no one deceive you with empty words

65

~ IX ~

a light unto my path

73

~ X ~

honey and milk are under your tongue

84

~ XI ~

i create light...

96

~ XII ~

...and create darkness

107

~ XIII ~

and death shall be no more

124

everything, as always, for aarti

for ryan, nate, and aj,
who tried to make this a religion

~ I ~

BEHOLD, THE NEW HAS COME

And what rough beast, its hour come round at last, slouches towards Bethlehem to be born?

With trembling hands covered in blood, the priest rose from her knees. Automatically, she fell into her routine. She cleansed herself and her tools.

She tried not to think about the blood.

She placed a blend of mugwort, lavender, and juniper into the censer and lit the fire. She entered the sanctuary and crossed it seven times, swinging the censer as she walked.

She tried not to think about the blood.

She set her tools down on the altar one by one, to reconsecrate them; a crucifix, stakes, a mallet, rosary, and a pistol. She removed the gloves from the interior pocket of her cassock and slid the delicate wool over her scarred hands. Tenderly, she lifted each tool and dipped it in the chalice filled with holy water, praying over it before setting it back in its place.

She tried not to think about the blood.

The first rays of sunrise began to filter through the stained glass, sending an ocean of blue and green sprinkling across the room. Reflexively, she jerked away from the uncomfortable light and made to shutter the windows, sealing her in darkness once more. She would need to sleep before she offered her services to her parishioners later in the afternoon. She ascended the stairs hidden off to the side of the sanctuary to her room, where she knew she would be safe from the sun, and her parishioners would be safe from her.

And all Sera could dream about was the blood.

~ II ~

BE RENEWED IN THE SPIRIT
OF YOUR MIND

The blood, which had plagued Sera for more of her waking hours than she cared to admit, was a problem that could be easily solved. If she abstained for too long, even the blood of her kin that she culled from the earth became mouth-wateringly tantalizing, as it had after her most recent encounter. It was only then that she would dream of the stuff, of tearing the world asunder and bathing in an endless flowing river of crimson. However, if she kept busy she barely had time to notice the gnawing feeling in her chest.

She awoke, as always, in a prison of her own making. As she had made her way to her bed at sunrise, she had opened the curtain on the window adjacent from her unadorned bed. Sunlight could fill every part of her room save for the corner in which her bed was tucked away. In the event that she ever awoke before the sun had properly set in a state of hunger-fueled disorientation, the failsafe would end her reign of terror before it could begin.

But she awoke right when she should, to the ringing of her church's small bell. She had hired a young girl to, among other things, climb the belltower to ring it precisely at 6pm each day. The girl - Kya, her name was - took care of the grounds during the days. It was a small job, but one she did dutifully.

Sera slid from her bed and turned to the crucifix on the wall opposite her bed, kneeling down as close to it as she could stand. Here she clasped her hands and bowed her head in prayer. She typically rotated between several, and the latest prayer she sought comfort in was one she often turned to when she needed the strength to abstain.

"'For the life of the flesh is in the blood, and I have given it to you on the altar to make atonement. For it is the blood by reason of the life that makes atonement'," she recited. "'You are not to eat the blood of any flesh, for the life of all flesh is its blood; whoever eats it shall be cut off.' If it is not your will to remove this curse, grant your humble servant the strength to overcome these sinful desires."

As usual, she took a few breaths that she didn't need and waited to see if her god would be moved enough to free her. But, as usual, nothing happened.

Sera got dressed as neatly as she could in the shadows of her room. Though she could see perfectly well in the darkness, the lack of a reflection forced her to rely on routine to ensure she was proper. She made her way back down to the chapel to start her day. Her days - or afternoons, rather - began with late Mass. The people were grateful when she first came to town, offering to hold services later in the day. Try as they might, the devout citizens of Gònghé Chéngshì still had lives to live, and the secular world very rarely understood their need for time off. The small group of faithful parishioners who attended her services when she first showed up grew with each service and continued to grow over the months until they resurrected the dingy old church. Its wooden pews were still filled with splinters and some attendees would complain about a draft here and there, but it was still the nicest set up she'd ever had.

Sera appreciated the routine provided by Mass; the Gloria, the liturgies, and the prayers always flowed beautifully from one to the other, their lifted spirits undaunted by the darkening sky. After Mass, most of the parishioners filtered out after congregating for a bit. On occasion, there were one or two stragglers - one who wanted to bask in the residual glory for a bit longer, and one who needed her help. It was always easy to tell which was which. One usually had their head leaned back in ecstasy, tears free falling as their burdens were lifted. The other was usually doubled over, nervously trying to make eye contact with the priest.

Sera affixed a warm smile once she caught his eye and slowly made her way over to where he sat in one of the very last pews.

"Something tells me you might need a listening ear," she said. She gestured to the empty space next to him, arching a brow. "May I sit?"

"It's, uh, your church, Father," he responded.

Sera chuckled quietly as she sat. "Are you finding the church to your liking?"

He let out a harried breath and gripped the pew in front of him. "I'm trying to. I haven't been having the easiest time lately. It seems like it's problem after insurmountable problem, if I'm being honest. There's no end in sight. I've lost everything, and my faith is the next to go. I work in the mornings, so when I heard there was a church here in Republic City that held services in the afternoon, I decided to make the journey."

"'When you pass through the waters, I will be with you; and when you pass through the rivers, they will not sweep over you. When you walk through the fire, you will not be burned; the flames will not set you ablaze'," Sera recited. "Things always seem more difficult when we feel as if we're on our own, but you're never alone. It might not seem like it now, but our father would never forsake one of his own."

He nodded as Sera spoke, keeping his eyes on the pews in front of him. "What's the point of me suffering, anyway? Why do I feel so alone if I'm not?"

"I like to look at it this way - he already knows what you can and can't handle. He's not going to put you in the path of something that is beyond your capabilities. He already knows your strength, but he wants you to be able to see that strength yourself."

"Am I really that strong if I'm struggling with my faith?"

"There were more prophets who questioned his plans than those whose faith never wavered," Sera grinned, earning a small smile from her charge. "It's not the destination that matters so much as the journey. And, personally, I believe those who struggle tend to come out the other side with a much stronger relationship."

He paused to consider her words for a moment, to let them truly sink in. Then he moved his hand in what Sera assumed was going to be a handshake, but a splinter from the back of the wooden pew caught in his finger. Before Sera could say anything, he immediately plucked the large obtrusion from his skin with a swear under his breath.

Blood bubbled up from the broken skin.

Almost as if pulled backwards by some external force, Sera flung herself to the opposite side of the pew. Her back hit the arm at the end, but she barely registered it pressing against her cassock. The parishioner looked at her in surprise and confusion, raising his hands.

"Hey, I'm real sorry for swearing," he said, his voice high. "I've been meaning to work on that."

Sera forced herself to maintain eye contact with him as she gripped onto the pew underneath her, trying with all her might not to look at the small speck of blood still present on his finger.

"No, it's not that," she grunted out. "I-I just didn't realize how late it was getting. It's dark out, and there's no one around."

It's dark out, and there's no one around.

"I have a few more things to take care of here before I lock up," Sera continued, desperate to keep her voice from trembling. It wasn't working, because he was looking at her with more concern than confusion. "Will you be able to make it home safely?"

"Uh, yeah," he replied, getting to his feet. "Are you okay, Father?"

It's dark out, and there's no one around.

"I'm fine," she managed to grunt out. "Please, if there's nothing else pressing on your mind, you really must be going."

He hesitated as if he was going to bring something else up, and Sera prayed that he would simply leave it at that. Her prayers were answered this time, because he nodded and turned to leave. It was only when the stone doors closed behind him that Sera's grip on the pew got so tight that a chunk of the seat broke off in her hand. When she expected to be around blood, she could prepare herself for the smell of it, for the way the sin of desire called out to her. But something so sudden and unexpected wore on her self-control - she clasped her free hand over her mouth as she felt her canines elongating, far beyond her control. She stumbled as she rose to her feet, tripping over them. She needed to make it to her room where she kept blood for situations like these. The blood, stolen from a nearby hospital, was long dead, but the repulsive stuff was what she survived off of. Nothing would compare to the way fresh blood tasted. She could never allow herself to give in to that temptation no matter how *deep* the ache inside of her ran, no matter how the beast within would remind her of how the adrenaline of the hunt made her feel closest to her god, how there was just as much divinity in death as there was in life, how --

The creak of the church's entrance sounded.

Sera whipped her head around, and there he was again, closing the door behind him with a sheepish expression on his face.

"I'm sorry, Father," he began. "I did have one more question."

He would never get to ask it. She descended on him before she could even think to stop herself. She hadn't given her feet the command to move, and yet she found herself beside the poor man with one hand grasping the hair on the back of his head and the other covering his mouth just as he tried to scream.

"I'm sorry," she echoed back to him before the ravenous beast consumed her.

She yanked his head to the side roughly and sunk her teeth in. The force of the impact punctured that throbbing vein in his neck, and blood sprayed into Sera's mouth quicker than she could swallow. A part of her noted how feebly he tried to push her off of him, how his hands grappled for purchase against her black suit. If she stopped now, he might be able to survive. She could make him forget what she had done. She'd already taken enough to sate the hunger for a time. She needed to stop. His pulse was getting weaker. Why couldn't she stop?

Her vision blurred as the beast within forced her to bring his body closer to her as they slid down to the wooden floors together, creaking under their combined weight. She held him in an intimate and tender embrace, unable to stop herself even as blood dribbled down her chin. He still tried to fight, his hands repeatedly landing gently against her face until they were coated in his own blood. The stream of blood eventually slowed, and his hands went still.

Sera let out a strangled cry as the beast finally released her from its clutches, her head thrown back in a sob. Her head swam between equally overwhelming warring feelings of guilt and ecstasy washing over her. With every breath she took, she could feel her high rising until she slumped back against the nearest pew with her eyes closed, the pale corpse resting peacefully in her lap.

"That was quite a show." A high voice called out from the front of the church.

Sera rose to her feet so fast that the body ungracefully thumped against the floor. She readied herself to have to kill whoever the innocent witness was, knowing there was no use in attempting to lie. But what she saw, sitting on the altar with her legs dangling, was far from innocent.

"What are you doing here?" She narrowed her eyes. "I told you that you weren't welcome here, Inaka."

Inaka grinned.

~ III ~

TO THE DEPTHS OF THE PIT

The head of the oldest coven, and herself one of the oldest of their kin in existence, Inaka Sato was a force to be reckoned with. All pencil skirts, nylon stockings, and ball gowns, every action she took exuded this fact. She feared next to nothing, not even sunlight - she was far too old for it to have any adverse effect on her. She was old enough to remember when vampires lived in the Second Realm, before The Cataclysm, before the gods disappeared, before they needed blood to survive.

Inaka used a gloved hand to precariously pick out the crucifix on the altar. She crossed one of her high-heeled legs over the other, shifting so that her skirt kept her thighs covered. "I've always known you were a glutton for punishment, Sera, but must you keep on with this nonsense? Do you know how annoying it is to have to protect you?"

"I don't need your protection," Sera replied. Her head still swam from the blood, and she wavered on her feet slightly. "I've never asked you for your help. In fact, I've told you to stay away from me and my church on multiple occasions."

"Then who would be here to clean up your messes?" Inaka tsked, nodding her head at Sera's victim, motionless on the floor.

Sera winced and removed her cassock, ignoring the bloodstains drying across the chest of her white collared shirt. She knelt on one knee, draped the black fabric over the poor soul, and prayed over his body. With any luck, her god would heed her prayer this time. The man she killed deserved to be at peace, to know that he hadn't been alone during his fight. If she knew how to summon one of the angels just to make sure he got that assurance, she would, but they would sooner kill her than help her.

"You know as well as I do that you can't go without a coven for much longer," Inaka warned. "It's nothing short of a miracle that you've gone this long undetected. I would absolutely hate to see anything happen to you."

Sera's head whipped up from where she knelt, green eyes glaring daggers. "You keep sending your minions after me and I'll keep killing them."

Inaka sighed and set the crucifix down. "It pains me that you see me as some sort of tyrant. You could just tell them no, you know."

"I was sending you a message."

"What you're doing is acting like a child. And you haven't been a child for well over a century now. Isn't that right, Father?"

Sera clenched her jaw and picked the body up into her arms effortlessly. While one of the doors adjacent to the sanctuary led to her bedroom, the other led outside. About a mile or so beyond the church was its dilapidated graveyard, and that was where she intended to lay this soul to rest. "I'm going to bury him out back. I want you to be gone by the time I return."

"Fair enough. I only came here to formally request your appearance." Inaka fished around in the pocket of her fitted suede coat and retrieved some rolled up paper. She held it up and let it unfurl, revealing a poster. Sera rolled her eyes and began walking for the exit as Inaka continued speaking. "Though I'd like for you to join my Guàiwù, I understand that you're stubborn. But I will no longer be looking out for you. If you don't join a coven this year, The Organization will find out, and they won't be happy."

With an unhelpful wink, Inaka disappeared in a mist of smoke, leaving behind the poster in her place.

Sera took a deep breath and searched for her patience, somewhere deep inside of her. Even if Inaka hadn't said anything, the mere presence of her sire would have been enough to call out to the beast within. She needed to be in a reverent state of mind. She looked down at the body in her arms; the cassock had fallen from her victim's face in death, and a fresh wave of guilt pushed through all other emotions. He would have looked so peacefully asleep were it not for the blood, puncture marks, and how unnervingly pale he was.

"'He will wipe away every tear from their eyes, and death shall be no more'," she began, whispering as she exited the chapel into the dark of the night. "'Neither shall there be mourning, nor crying, nor pain anymore, for the former things have passed away.'"

Sera recited this repeatedly as she slowly made her way to the graveyard, shrouded in darkness and covered by a small forest of thick gingko trees. The air felt tense, like it was going to rain soon. She came to the edge of the plot of land and set the body down. Then she got down on her hands and knees and began to dig, all the while repeating the verse. She gently lowered the body into its grave and covered it up. Then she searched the surrounding grounds for anything large enough to memorialize his death, to honour the fact that he had existed, to leave something behind that his mourning family wouldn't even know existed. She knew she was doing it just to alleviate some of her guilt, but she persisted and she cast a blind eye to the other shallow graves without headstones. All that she could find that was even remotely suitable was a piece of someone else's headstone that had been chipped off and left on the ground, likely by local grave-robbers. She wasn't sure what they thought they would ever find, but in the short months she'd been in town she'd had to chase off a fair amount of them.

"'And the dust returns to the earth as it was, and the spirit returns to the god who gave it'," Sera said as she pressed the headstone piece into the ground. She grabbed her cassock from the ground and slung it over her shoulder, kneeling down over the grave. If this were a funeral she were presiding over, she would have the family say something about the deceased. This typically went on for a little bit, and Sera could almost feel as if she were a part of the family herself. Then she would give a short sermon and provide counseling for the family. But she was alone, and she knew nothing about the person she killed.

She turned her head towards the sky as the first droplets of rain fell, and then it turned into a sudden downpour. Still she remained, kneeling down in the graveyard with her head tilted back. She wished she was strong enough to plead for her guilt to be washed away if her god wasn't going to take this curse away from her. But she knew she deserved it. For not being strong enough, for worshiping the wrong god, for having ever welcomed the curse in the first place.

Later, she would instead be grateful that she had fed.

If she hadn't, she wouldn't have smelled the moment when someone entered the forest behind the church. And she wouldn't have smelled it when, a mere second later, that strange someone entered the vicinity of the graveyard and launched a volley of sharpened stakes directly at her chest. With blood-fueled speed, she reflexively snatched one of the stakes from the air and flung it towards her attacker. Had Inaka sent more of her minions after all? Were they intent on getting revenge for their fallen siblings? But those questions were quickly put to rest; the stake Sera returned to its sender scratched her assailant's face, and the blood she smelled was nothing like she had ever experienced before. It certainly wasn't human. Another second later, she saw their face.

Her assailant had horns protruding from their temple, a thick, prehensile tail, red skin with black markings, and sharpened claws that were poised to strike. Sera grabbed her attacker by their wrists and used their momentum to fling them over and onto the ground, where she promptly straddled their waist. She drew a hand back, but her fist only hit muddied soil; her attacker slid from between her legs and Sera felt a strong foot kick against her back and sent her face down into the dirt. She rolled over just in time to avoid another stake from being plunged into her heart. Instead of getting back to her feet, she stayed low and kicked out their legs from under them, sending them slipping and stumbling backwards, losing their grip on the stake swallowed up by the mud. Sera freed the stake from its sheath and grabbed the attacker by their shirt before they had time to recover from being thrown off balance. Sera leveled the stake at her attacker's throat and slammed them into a tree, then another after her force caused the first tree to snap in half.

"Tell me who you are and who sent you and I will set you free," Sera said. "I don't want to kill you."

"*Potes meus suaviare clunes*," they spat, black blood landing squarely in the middle of Sera's face.

"Are they still teaching you hunters Latin?" Sera fought the urge to wipe the blood from her face. Instead, she pressed the stake against the skin of their throat.

"I'm not a hunter." They struggled to get out from under Sera's grip, but she could tell that they didn't expect to be fighting, nor did they have a plan to get away from her. All their stakes were out of their possession, and Sera couldn't feel the sensation that she got whenever she got too near a crucifix.

"What are you supposed to be?"

Instead of answering, they posed a question of their own. "December 4th, 1898. Did you kill Geng Zemin?"

Sera blinked, her grip on the shirt slackening ever so slightly. "How could you possibly know that?"

The being beneath her growled. "Answer the question."

Sera hesitated, giving her attacker all the confirmation they needed. For decades after she had been sired, she was at Inaka's beck and call. It was a role she went into willingly, just as she had willingly gone into death's embrace once it was offered to her. Where Inaka sent her, she went. Who she was told to kill, she killed without question. When the Guàiwù wanted to cut a red swathe across the mainland, she was there leading the charge. And if whole empires fell and regimes changed when they were done, Sera was too consumed by bloodlust to notice.

"You killed my mentor before he was done training me!" They yelled. "I've been trying to find you ever since. But when you split off from your coven and changed your life, it was like you had fallen from the face of earth entirely."

Sera arched a brow. "Are you what I think you are?"

"Are you what I *know* you are?" they retorted, angrily.

She, of course, knew about demons. How there had only ever been a handful of them, created by angels from dead human mages, each made for the express purpose of following orders. It wasn't that they couldn't think on their own, but rather that they were so goal oriented that it didn't often occur to them that they could do anything else. But as she had never met one before, she had long believed they were some myth created by humans that somehow got into the heads of supernaturals.

Sera shook her head, clearing it. If she got distracted, the demon would take the opportunity to fight again, and she wasn't looking forward to that prospect. "I need to know if you came alone."

"Why not just kill me now?"

"I don't want to kill you, truly. I just want to be safe. I want to be left alone."

"I saw all the blood in your church. I'm sure the person you killed wanted to feel safe as well," they sneered. "You pretend to be a priest. You've convinced these people to trust a monster."

"Don't say that." Sera pleaded, though she knew that's exactly what she was. "I didn't mean to kill him. I didn't want to."

"Well let's dig him up and ask what he wants!" The demon laughed, then coughed, blood coating their lips. It was only then that Sera noticed that a piece of the tree had splintered off and was coming out the other side through the demon's body, black blood coating their torso. She almost swore.

"You're hurt," she remarked, dropping the stake and kicking it further into the forest.

"You threw me all around this forest and you're surprised that I'm injured?"

Sera immediately broke the branch off and pulled it from the demon's body, wincing as they cried out in pain. She ripped off the hem of her shirt and wrapped it around their torso. The whole time, the demon feebly fought against her, feeling their own body down like they were looking for another weapon.

With an annoyed sigh, she grabbed hold of the demon's chin and forced them to make eye contact. She pushed past the strange feeling that she had seen those eyes before and said, "Stop fighting. I'm trying to help you."

Immediately, the demon went still as they obeyed Sera's command, another perk to being well and recently fed. Instead of dwelling on that powerful feeling surging in her veins, Sera picked the injured demon up into her arms, ignoring how the smell of demon blood was grossly unappetizing and nearly putrid smelling. She couldn't have another death on her hands, not so soon after the last.

So she brought the unconscious demon up to her room and laid them on her bed, sheets be damned. Sera kept a decently sized first aid kit in the old, dilapidated dresser in her room. It was primarily in case of emergencies in the church, but when she went without feeding for long enough, she found herself able to be injured. The prospect terrified her.

When she turned back to her bed, the demon was shifting, returning back into their human form; horns receding and skin patching up their points of exit, claws receding back to normal fingernails, skin colour changing from red to its natural hue. Sera wanted to look away, sure she was crossing some sort of line.

But then she realized the unconscious form began to look familiar. She blinked a few times, certain that there had to have been some mistake, that surely the form would keep shifting and form a face far less familiar. She took a few steps closer and looked down onto the sleeping form of the girl she had hired to assist in her church.

~ IV ~

THE OLD THINGS HAVE PASSED AWAY

Though she had seen the transformation with her own eyes, Sera couldn't wrap her mind around the fact that the young girl was the demon who had tried to kill her, who had wanted her dead, apparently, for the past forty-seven years. Did she know who Sera was the entire three weeks she had worked there?

As a child, Sera had been cast out by her parents for reasons she would never be able to comprehend. She had been made to wait on the doorstep of a temple on the mainland, and the priests there were kind enough to take her in. Rather than turning her over to become a ward of the state, she was raised there. She learned the ins and outs of how a church was run and learned from her rotating list of parental figures how a priest was meant to act. They trained her to follow in their footsteps. Humans were blissfully ignorant of just how insignificant they were. They had no awareness of the non-humans that walked among them, living their lives in plain sight. They believed themselves to be the only sentient beings on the planet, and believed their god to be the only one.

So did she, up until the moment she met Inaka.

Sera wasn't sure how to handle the situation. She couldn't kill the girl, but if she let her go, she would most certainly bide her time until she tried to kill Sera again. Sera would have to leave her church, leave the humans she had come to care for, and roam the earth until she felt safe again. No, for the time being she had to keep an eye on Kya, and the only way to do that was by keeping her close. But then the situation became one of figuring out how to keep the girl close without risking her life - the sun would come up eventually, and she would put something sharp through Sera's chest the moment she got the chance.

Sera made it to the small collection of books neatly packed away in the sanctuary in a second. The group of twenty books were her most prized possessions, stolen from a library buried in the sand on the other side of the continent. Several of them had been written by some human mage from ancient times by the name of Soleiman and one of them very specifically spoke on non-human creatures, including demons. She scanned the books until she found the leather-bound one that might have the answer she needed.

Kya was still unconscious when Sera returned seconds after she had left, and she didn't stir when Sera closed her bedroom door behind her. She flipped through pages upon pages detailing different ways to defend against and kill vampires, fairies, and shapeshifters until she got to the section on demons. The section began with diagrams of different types of demons with their body parts labelled and notes jotted down on them; some of them had claws and tails, some had wings, some looked humanoid and some didn't. Eventually, she flipped to the pages that described their known weaknesses. The most prominent of that was supposedly iron, as something with the metal interfered with the magic used to reanimate demons.

The next several pages described magical symbols that were alleged to do different things. Some of them killed the demon while others put the demon under the control of the person who drew the symbols. The one that caught Sera's eye, however, claimed that when it was drawn around a demon, it prevented them from leaving the space marked out by the symbols.

Sera flattened the book out on the ground and studied the symbols for a bit. She searched her desk for something to write with and came away with a thick piece of chalk. She got down on her hands and knees and drew several interlocking circles around her bed. Once those were done and connected, she added the necessary symbols to finish the binding and went over them several times until the white contrasted starkly with the dark wood in her room. When she was finished, she stood up straight and dusted her hands off.

Kya began to stir then. Sera stepped just outside of the binding circles and waited for her to fully regain consciousness. When she did, she bolted upright in the bed, squinting into the darkness.

"Where am I?" she asked, nearly yelling. "What are you going to do to me?"

"Please relax," Sera replied. "If I wanted you dead, I would have let you die. I saved your life."

"I suppose you expect me to be grateful?"

"I don't expect anything from you aside from answers to some questions I have."

Kya scoffed. "What makes you think I'll answer you? How are you so sure I won't kill you the first chance I get?"

"I'm not sure you can," Sera said, arching a brow. She wasn't completely certain that those drawings would even work; human mages were great at deceiving others, so there was a chance that the book was full of nonsense.

But Kya seemed to take this as a challenge, as she growled in response. "You should have killed me when you had the chance."

Kya sprung up out of the bed, and Sera instinctively squatted as she readied herself into a fighting stance. But instead of attacking, Kya looked down at the ground underneath her, standing directly on one of the symbols etched into the ground. Then her eyes fell on the book by Sera's feet.

"Clever," Kya sighed. She walked the length of the bed and came to the edge of the binding. She held up a hand and prodded the invisible barrier. No matter how much force Kya applied, something unseen moved against her, keeping her bound. "So now I'm your prisoner? Is this your way of proving to me that you're not a monster?"

"You worked for me for weeks. You were even at a few of my services. Was there anything I did that made you feel as if I was inauthentic?"

"So the monster doesn't believe she's a monster," Kya scoffed. She sat back down on the bed and untied the bloodied strip of shirt Sera had compressed her wound with, revealing freshly healed light brown skin. "That doesn't change what you are, *Father*."

Sera ran her fingers through her still wet hair and sighed. She couldn't keep the girl captive forever - keeping her until tomorrow night probably would be too risky anyway. The room wasn't soundproof, and she would probably scream the moment parishioners came into the church at sunset the next day.

Which reminded Sera that there was still blood in the chapel.

"I have to go take care of something," Sera said. "Please make yourself as comfortable as possible." And as she left the room, she couldn't help but look over her shoulder with a small smirk to add, "Try not to go anywhere."

The ghost of a smile disappeared once she returned to the chapel and looked at all the blood, concentrated between the last few pews and the door. It wasn't much of a mess, but over the past few hours it had dried and made the scene look that much more eerie. If this was what Kya had walked into, it was no small wonder that she saw Sera as a monster.

From the shed behind the church, Sera grabbed her cleaning supplies and got to work. She caught a glimpse of the poster Inaka had brought as she passed through to the back of the church. She opened the poster and rolled her eyes at how over-the-top it looked; the covens didn't get together outside of the annual event, but Sera had participated in enough to know before even reading it that les Infernaux Noirs would be in charge of it this year. She hadn't been to such an event in decades, but she could tell that it would only be more decadent than years past. As humans grew more gaudy and advanced, so too did the non-human society.

When she was done cleaning up her mess, Sera locked the church doors, condemning it to disuse once more. She would only be fooling herself if she thought she could stay in the city for much longer. People would eventually go looking for the person she had killed, and someone would remember that he came to her church. They would ask around, people would eventually realize that he stayed back when everyone else left the church, and suspicion would be cast on her. She would be safe if she joined Inaka's coven, but if Kya tried to track her down, any attack on her life would make her a target. Even if she had tried to kill her, Sera had grown somewhat fond of the girl when she worked for her, and didn't want to see any harm come to her. There had to be a solution to this dilemma.

But she feared that solution would have to involve Inaka.

~ V ~

IN YOU I TAKE REFUGE

It was nearing midnight, and they hadn't made any headway.

Sera sat on the floor across from her bed, taking the time to study more of the human mage's writings. She sighed as she turned another page going in depth into the biology of the different types of tails demons could possess. There were a few items described in the book that she had set up on her desk; a bowl of salt, fresh mugwort, and a small clipping of rosemary.

"I'm not going anywhere with you," Kya said simply but firmly, sitting upright in Sera's bed. Her tattered shirt revealed that her wound had fully healed, and she sat gazing out the window into the darkness.

"I don't think you understand that I'm doing this for your own good," Sera said, keeping her eyes on the faded drawing. "Let me make it clear. You don't trust me. You'll probably try to kill me the first chance you get. I don't want you dead, even if you don't want to believe me. My only logical option is to bring you with me and let someone else figure out what to do with you."

"And you plan to bring me to a gathering of several thousand vampires."

"Do you not think I can protect you?"

"What reason do you have to keep me safe?"

Sera looked up at the girl on her bed and arched a brow, as if the answer was obvious. "I have no reason to wish you harm."

Kya made a face. "I just tried to kill you."

Sera shrugged and leaned her head back against the wall she was sitting against. "'For if you forgive other people when they sin against you, your heavenly father will also forgive you.'"

"Ah, the virtuous vampire," Kya scoffed. "And you expect me to not only trust you, but trust whoever you're planning to hand me off to?"

"I'm not *handing you off* to anyone. There's someone there who can help us both."

"Right," Kya said, gesturing with her hands. "I'm supposed to trust you, you're supposed to trust me, and we're both supposed to trust the person who was a monster before The Cataclysm even happened."

"I would like you to come with me willingly. I certainly can make you, but I wanted to give you a chance to play nice."

At that, Kya's bravado faded and she fell back against the headboard of the bed with her arms crossed over her chest, frowning. Sera couldn't help but feel a pang in her chest. She didn't want to compel Kya, but the girl wasn't giving her much of a choice. Moving solely under cover of darkness, it would take them weeks of traveling to make it to the city les Infernaux Noirs was holding the event in. Her compulsion would wear unless she fed again.

That would be a problem for later Sera.

She got to her feet and drew out a large leather suitcase from under her bed, packed neatly for a situation like this in which she had to run away from her church. She had hoped that the day she needed to use this would never come, but she had been realistic. She retrieved the books and her holy scriptures and placed them all reverently in her suitcase. From her dresser she grabbed two extra cassocks and more plain collared shirts. This place wasn't home - she feared she would never find home again - but it still hurt her to have to leave it behind. If Kya hadn't caught her, she could have stayed until something else forced her out. That's just the way her world worked.

"How do you plan to force me to cooperate?" Kya asked, looking up at her from where she lay.

"The same way as before, if you won't play nice," Sera said. "There's also another binding in that book that will make you have to listen to me, but that's much more permanent. I'm hoping that it won't need to come to that, though. I pray that on this journey, you learn to trust me. Or at least you don't try to kill me."

She offered Kya a hesitant smile. Kya spat at her again.

"Well," Sera sighed and pinched the bridge of her nose. "I would like to be as ethical as possible. I'll only ever compel you to do the same two things; stay by my side and don't try to hurt me. Compulsion wears off, so I'll have to do it a few times while we travel, but I'll warn you beforehand each time. Like now, for example."

Before Kya could blink, or had time to realize what was happening, Sera crossed through the barrier and was by her side. She wrapped her fingers gently, but firmly, around Kya's jaw and tilted her head back, peering down into her piercing blue eyes. And with a strong voice, Sera commanded, "You don't want to hurt me. You'll stay by my side as we travel."

Kya's pupils dilated for a moment as the compulsion set in, working its way through her mind. Sera released Kya's jaw and put her hands behind her back. She took a few steps back, grabbing the piece of chalk from her desk with one hand, bunched up in the same hand that held a small scrap of paper. Her other hand deftly scooped up a handful of salt, which she cautiously spread over one of the outlines she had drawn on the floorboards, effectively neutralizing the binding. Kya got to her feet almost instinctively and took a few steps past the newly created opening and Sera fell backwards against her desk. She knew she should be drawing that binding symbol that would force Kya to obey her, but she held out hope that the compulsion would stick as it had before, that Kya's own will didn't overpower it.

Kya's brows furrowed in confusion as she looked down at Sera, her mouth opening and closing repeatedly before she seemed to collect her bearings. She put some distance between them, shaking her head.

"Well, what are you waiting for?" Kya asked. "We have somewhere to be, and one of us can't travel during daylight."

****

When they first left the church, Kya suggested they burn it down. That way, if anyone should come looking for Sera or the man she killed, there would be no evidence of either of them having been there.

Sera nipped that idea in the bud.

While they ran, she'd had to slow down to ensure Kya could keep up, and they took frequent breaks. Sera didn't know if it was a demon thing or a Kya thing, but the girl had short bursts of speed that needed a similar amount of time to regenerate. Though she didn't expect to see much of the girl again once they reached the Coven gathering, Sera couldn't help but catalogue each new thing she learned. According to the book, demons could choose their demon form once they were reanimated. As they were made by Passio's league of angels, passion ruled them, and their forms were often directly influenced by what they were made to do - demons who were made to help keep the peace typically had wings while those who were made for vengeance had skin like blood. Like Kya's demon form.

They ran until Sera found a suitable motel to wait the day out at, about an hour before sunrise. The small motel was out of the way, and Sera would have assumed it was empty had it not been for the candlelights in the window. The building looked as if it had been built the year Sera was born; it held a compact lounging area with a handful of circular tables and scattered chairs, a long bench situated against a wall with a hooded patron asleep at it. The whole lobby had a faint smell of a forest, though there wasn't one nearby. The woman at the front desk tried to sell them drinks that they denied, and had provided each room with a bowl of fruit that looked like they would soon mold. Their room was simply furnished; it had two twin beds, a desk, and a chair for the desk. The person at the front desk took one look at Sera's cassock and assured her that she wouldn't have to pay for the lodging, which was a relief. The little money she had brought would be for emergencies and things like buying Kya food.

"Aren't you hungry?" Sera asked, shoving her suitcase under her bed. "What do you eat?"

"What, it doesn't say anything about that in that book of yours?" Kya snarked.

Sera sighed as she closed the blinds on the room's two windows. "So far, no. I've just read that there are different types of demons. It's really droning on about the different ways your kind can look. And, of course, how to kill you."

"And how exactly do you plan to kill me?"

"The information is there, girl. It doesn't mean I plan to put it to use."

Kya rolled her eyes. "I was human, once. Most of me still is. I eat the same things they do, just not as often."

Sera removed her shoes and sat back on the small bed, stretching out. "Do you remember it? Being human?"

"Do you?"

They sat in silence for a bit. Sera hadn't been human since 1818, when Inaka found the then twenty-five year old and ended her life. Humanity was more than a century away and felt like little more than a memory. Sure, Sera could remember the details of her human life, but it felt as detached as if she were watching a film. There were no emotions aligned to these memories of someone who had died long ago; Sera the human was simply a part of the collective past.

"Yes," Sera responded finally. "But I don't feel anything for it. There's no deep, melancholy desire to return to a life I can never have again."

"You're lucky," Kya eventually said, just as Sera was fading in and out of sleep. "I woke up in this body with all these emotions and feelings with no memories behind them. I don't know anything about who she was."

***

When Sera woke up, there was a paper sticking to her forehead.

Out looking for food. -K

A part of her wondered if her compulsion had worn off. Sera wondered if it would be such a bad thing. She wouldn't have to see Inaka. She could stay at the motel with free room and board. The person at the desk seemed receptive; she could offer services to those who wanted it and make a home here for however long she could manage it. There had to be a decent hospital nearby that she could volunteer at in order to re-up her supply of blood. If Kya had actually left to lick her wounds and prepare to fight Sera another day, she probably wouldn't expect Sera to stay in this dingy motel in the middle of nowhere. It would be boring, but it would be peaceful.

But first, Sera had to know whether or not Kya was still there.

The dark light pressing against the blinds of the windows let her know that the dangers of the day were long gone. Sera had slept in her pants and white shirt, so she pulled on one of her spare cassocks and flattened out any wrinkles before leaving the room. The lobby looked the same as it had when they arrived the previous night, except there was a different person at the main desk. That hooded patron was still seated at a table with food, except there was someone enjoying their company.

Surprising herself, Sera smiled when she saw Kya talking around a mouthful of food.

Sera shook her head - Kya only stayed because she compelled her to, not because the girl felt any sort of camaraderie. Kya looked up and waved Sera forward, speaking when the latter took a seat across from the pair.

"My new friend here said she had one of those wheeled contraptions *people* use to get around and she'd be willing to take us where we need to go," Kya said, waving her hand as she spoke. A handful of bills she must have taken from Sera while she slept was laid flat out on the table. "It's *completely covered* and has *tinted windows*."

Sera wondered if Kya had always been this subtle.

Said friend turned to face Sera, removing her hood. Her eyes were a peculiar shade of dark green. A strangely familiar green. "Well I gots to admit I didn't expect your traveling partner to be a priestly dame, but whatever you two get up to in the back-seat is your business."

Sera tilted her head in confusion while Kya's cheeks lit up. She choked on her food. "Oh, you've got this all wrong," Kya said with a nervous laugh. "We're not trying to -"

Green Eyes raised her hand and chuckled, shaking her head. As she did, Sera got another whiff of forest, as if the woman before her had just gone for a run and brushed up against every single leaf she could find. "I don't want to know your business, I just want your business, get it?"

"Wait a minute," Sera said, narrowing her eyes. "I thought the motel just had a strange smell, but it's coming from you."

"Don't be rude," Kya chastised her.

But Sera made eye contact with Kya's new friend and searched them, leaning in close and lowering her voice. "I'm willing to bet Green Eyes here doesn't always look like this. Care to show us what you really are?"

The woman across from her winked. A hand shot out to grab the cash off the table, and she went out the door. Sera wanted to run after her, but a quick glance behind her showed that their little party had attracted the attention of the person at the desk. She didn't want to attract any more unnecessary attention.

"What just happened?" Kya asked, looking between the escape route and Sera, brows thick with confusion.

"I take it you've never encountered a shapeshifter before," Sera sighed. She sat up straight and pinched the bridge of her nose. "Please tell me that wasn't all of my money."

Kya smiled apologetically.

The evening of the last day of their trip, Sera could feel her strength waning. She'd been compelling Kya when she awoke every evening. She'd never stuck around someone she'd compelled for very long, so she had no idea exactly when compulsion wore off, but knew that it would at some point.

"I hope you understand that this is just for safety," Sera said, looking down at the handcuffs in her lap. With a sharp switchblade in hand, she etched those binding symbols into each of the handcuffs. "You don't smell like one of us. I have to protect you."

Kya scoffed. She spun back and forth in the rolling chair situated in the corner of their latest room, refusing to look at Sera. "And how exactly is this protecting me? Isn't controlling my mind enough?"

Sera winced. She knew that was what she was doing, there wasn't a doubt about it, but she hated thinking about it that way. "My kin are rather fond of hierarchies. It won't take long for someone to notice that you're not one of us, and they'll try to, ah, control you unless you look like you're already under someone's control."

Kya stopped spinning and placed her feet firmly on the floor. But before she could spew whatever hurtful statement she was about to make, Sera spoke up.

"It's only until we find Inaka," Sera assured her, looking up to see the hateful look in Kya's eyes. "Once she hears that I'm there, she'll find us soon enough."

"Then we can go our separate ways?"

"Then we can go our separate ways," Sera confirmed.

"And I can have my mind back?"

"And you can have your mind back."

Kya paused to think it over, as if it was an offer and as if she had a choice. Eventually, she held out her wrists.

~ VI ~

BAD COMPANY RUINS GOOD MORALS

08 February 1818
Sera was up before the sun was, and she watched its zenith as it climbed into the sky. She let the warmth wash over her, then prepared for the days' events. Today was the day she had been looking forward to for weeks; it was the day Father Baoten would allow her to work the confessional after the church service. To the background of the hundreds in the congregation singing the glories of their blessed god Pario and all he did for them, she watched herself in the mirror as she got dressed. She buckled her freshly ironed pants, buttoned her collared white shirt, and slipped her cassock on. Her reflection showed her the perfect and pristine image of the priesthood. She had gotten dressed and tried on the outfit in this very mirror countless times before, but this would be the first time she got to wear it around people outside of her family.

Today was the day she would be able to begin helping people.

"Bless me Father for I have sinned," her first charge began. "It has been two weeks since my last confession."

"What would you like to share?" Sera asked.

"I have let hate fester in my heart, Father," he continued. "I received word that the army that occupies my homeland has gotten more bold and have taken more ground just as recently as last month. I find myself wishing the worst of things upon them. I have recently read things that stir me, that inject dark thoughts in my mind that I do not have the strength to fight off on my own."

As he continued to speak, Sera listened solemnly. She heard the pain and sadness in his voice and felt for him. It was so easy for people to fall into the traps of sin, and much more difficult to seek help when it was needed. When he was finished, she assigned him a penance and led him in a prayer of contrition.

"My god Pario, I am sorry for my sins with all my heart. In choosing to do wrong and failing to do good, I have sinned against you whom I should love above all things. I firmly intend, with your help, to do penance, to sin no more, and to avoid whatever leads me to sin. My god, have mercy," They both spoke.

Sera could hear the relief plain in his voice. "Go and sin no more."

The next few confessions went just as smoothly. She found herself spending longer with each person than she absolutely needed to, getting to know each sinner who stopped by. It was hard for her not to, difficult for her to remain completely impartial. She wanted to provide for these people, to reach out to them and change them for the better.

The sound of heels clicking across the floor making their way to her confessional booth captured Sera's attention. The door on the opposite side opened, someone entered, and closed it behind them.

"Bless me Father for I have sinned. It has been, oh, several years since my last confession," she said.

Sera felt a pang in her heart; she couldn't imagine going that long without talking to someone about the sinful thoughts that plagued her mind. This woman had to have been very strong to have kept the faith undeterred this long.

"What would you like to share?" Sera asked.

The sliding window between them that kept them separate and maintained the illusion of anonymity slid aside. With a surprised gasp, Sera turned to look at the opened partition. Her eyes grew wide with shock.

"Y-you're her," she said with a trembling voice. "The woman from my nightmares."

The black haired woman rested her arms on the divider and placed her head in her hand. She grinned over at Sera as if she had just found something priceless and worthwhile. "It's good to finally meet you."

"What do you mean 'finally'?"

The woman laughed, and the sound of it wholly thrilled and wholly terrified Sera.

"I have been awaiting you for a rather long while now, Father. Don't you think it's time you came home to me?"

"Excuse me?" Sera squeaked, her voice small. "Do you need to have someone walk you home? Are you in need of medical attention?"

"Silly girl," the woman chuckled as she leaned back, away from the partition. "You're even more beautiful up close."

Sera fought off a blush and reached for the sliding window to close it. "I-If you would like to set up a study session with one of our priests to receive his holy word-"

The woman propped her hand up and stopped the partition from moving. "Your god would not want to hear from me."

Her *god*?

"Pario's blessings are for everyone," Sera shook her head. "If you would allow me to--"

"I'll be back to see you next week, Father."

And with that, the nightmare woman closed the partition between them and exited the confessional booth. Sera could only lean back in her chair and wonder if they should put a knight or two at the door as security.

***

The entire event was to be held in a deep cavern underground. Its wide entrance on the side of a mountain quickly opened to reveal a limestone cavern thirty meters tall and illuminated in sparkling hues of green and blue. The further the pair walked, the darker the cavern grew, until only those who could see perfectly well in the dark could follow the path along the floor of the cave. They followed twists and turns for what felt like an entire day in complete darkness until the trail began to curve downwards. The trail ended abruptly with a twenty foot drop, and light exploded up to meet them once their feet hit the bottom.

No one quite threw a party like les Infernaux Noirs.

It looked more like a human carnival. The scene went on for what looked like miles, with colourful tents and shops stretching as far back as Sera could see. But instead of rides and carnival games, there were fabric shops and blood bars.

Sera took a deep breath and ignored the burning ache in her throat.

There was a line before them queueing up to the entrance of the event, a thick velvet separating those who had not checked in with those who took part in the celebrations. In front of the velvet line was a long row of what Sera could only assume were werewolves, all of a similarly muscular build with hair covering what skin was exposed. They stood stoically with their arms behind their backs, looking out over the crowd and scanning it for any sign of danger. Kya stood close to Sera, peering among the celebrants with obvious distrust on her face. The line progressed until they were face to face with the leader of les Infernaux Noirs, Mathis Berengar. He wore a veil over his dark skin, and his consorts stood on either side of him.

"*Bienvenue à notre événement,*" Mathis began. "*Nous espérons que vous l'apprécierez. Avec quel clan es-tu?*"

"I am not a part of any coven," Sera mumbled. "You can call me Sera."

"*Et qui est ton jouet apprivoisé?*"

Sera winced and prayed that Kya couldn't understand French. "She is just my companion. You don't need her name."

Matthais looked her over and, after a brief moment, stepped aside to let them pass. Sera let out a sigh of relief and waved Kya forward.

"What was that about?" Kya asked in a whisper, eyes narrowed as she looked around at the over the top display.

"The less my kin know about you, the better," Sera told her, shaking her head.

"I'll take your word for it," Kya raised her handcuffed hands and arched a brow. "Does that mean these can come off now?"

"Only if you understand that if you try to run or attack anyone, I'm the only one here who wouldn't try to hurt you."

Kya rolled her eyes and raised her hands again. Sera fished the key from her inner pocket and unlocked them. She sucked in a breath, catching the briefest glimpse of red, scarred outlines on Kya's wrists before she shoved her hands in her pockets.

"Thanks," Kya grumbled, pointedly refusing to make eye contact.

Before Sera could say anything further, she felt a tap on her shoulder. She turned around to see a woman shorter than she was, with glasses and hair pulled back into a sleek ponytail. On the third finger of her right hand was a large red carnelian ring, signifying her coven allegiance. Just behind her was a human, warm brown skin with an ashen tone to it, brown eyes that looked permanently glazed over, and a loosely fitting chain around her slender neck.

The woman in glasses bowed and smiled politely. "You're Sera, correct? I was sent to find you and bring you to my mistress."

That was faster than Sera expected. "Am I to assume this 'mistress' of whom you speak is Inaka Sato?"

"That is correct," the woman nodded. "My name is Nekiru Moon."

"Who's that behind you?" Kya asked.

Nekiru kept looking at Sera with that polite smile, as if Kya hadn't spoken.

"Oh, you've got to be fucking kidding me," Kya complained, throwing her hands up incredulously.

"Ah." Sera rubbed the back of her neck. "My frien- my companion here would like to know who the, um, young lady behind you is."

Nekiru raised a hand, and the woman - young girl, really - behind her came to her side, head bowed.

"Surely this must not surprise you, Sera. You know what these events are like. She is my *jouet apprivoisé*, my toy for the evening."

Sera could feel Kya's anger radiating off of her.

"Some of us like to frequent the blood bars, but I've chosen to just keep this one with me until I tire of her," Nekiru continued casually, as if someone's life did not hang on her whim. "You may partake as well, but we really must see Ms. Sato. For the sake of my companion and yours, we may take a speed befitting them."

Nekiru turned on her heel, as did the human beside her.

"I'll kill everyone in here," Kya growled from beside Sera. "Every last one of you."

"I doubt you would get very far," Sera told her, nodding towards Nekiru and her human's receding forms.

They walked through the bulk of the event grounds, passing tents for the other covens; Grave Rogues, la Myriade Tourmentée, Phantom Flight, Barakai, the Gauntlet, Sasabonsam, Lamashtu, Striges, Gallu, and of course, Inaka's Guàiwù. They each tried to appeal to the handful in the crowd who weren't attached to any coven, promising riches and land and - most important of all - fresh blood they wouldn't have to hunt for.

Nekiru stopped at a particular nondescript red tent and held it open for the pair to enter. There were rows and rows arranged like open confessionals with chairs on one side. Every chair had a human strapped down to it, each looking much more ecstatic than the last. Not all of the other sides of the rows were occupied, but the ones that were had the occasional vampire leaned back in a similar ecstasy, blood messily coating their mouths. Sera took a moment at the entrance and stopped breathing; it was a choice to breathe, and in a space like this it would only lead her further into temptation. She brought her hands together and dug her nails into either of her palms, the pain bringing clarity through the blood haze.

She caught sight of Inaka just as she moved to sit at one of the booths. The human opposite her was dark skinned and broad shouldered and had a lazy grin.

"Hi," the human breathed as they sat up, pushing their glasses further up their nose. "My name is-"

Inaka clucked her tongue and held up a hand. "No, thank you. I prefer it when my snacks don't speak to me."

From beside Sera, Kya spoke up. "Please tell me that's not her."

At this, Inaka turned to glance at them, a smile spreading across her face. "Ah, Sera. And Sera's....thing that I didn't know she was bringing. I'm so glad you took my advice. I'll be with you in just a moment."

Kya started forward, almost instinctively, and Sera threw out her hand to stop her. "Of all the battles you could pick, do *not* pick this one." Sera whispered.

They watched as the human tilted their head and bit their lip. Inaka grinned down at them and leaned forward, planting a chaste kiss against their neck and leaving behind a faint red outline. Her fangs shot out and she bit down. Sera looked away. Kya watched, shaking with anger.

Eventually, Inaka made her way over to them, sighing contentedly.

"It truly is a design flaw that we cannot get drunk on our own," she said as she approached, shaking her head. "But this makes up for it."

"Hello, Inaka," Sera sighed. "I need something from you."

"Whatever could that be, dearest?" Inaka replied.

"I need you to give me your word that you'll hear me out."

"For you? Anything."

Kya arched an accusing brow at Sera.

"My companion here is a demon. A vengeance demon, if I'm not mistaken." Sera gave Kya the chance to correct her. When she didn't, she continued. "She was determined to dispose of me because I killed her mentor at your behest. I don't want to cause her any more harm, so I'd like you to talk to the other coven leaders and make sure no one touches her. Even if, years from now, she comes back to finish the job she started. Even if she kills another of our kin."

Kya looked at her in surprise. Sera meant every word.

"I could do that," Inaka said, tilting her head. "But I am in the business of making deals. I will honour your request if you honour mine."

"What do you want?"

"Oh, Sera. You know what I want."

Sera bit her lip and dropped her gaze. Some small part of her had believed that the elder vampire would do something solely because she had asked her to.

"I am here, after all," Sera said to the ground. "I'll join your Guàiwù."

Inaka tilted her head up, a long, manicured finger under her chin. She gazed down into Sera's eyes with all the love and care one could afford a prized toy. "'Whom have I in all the realms but you? Earth has nothing I desire besides you'." She leaned down to whisper into Sera's ear. "Aren't you pleased that I learned scripture for you, *Father*?"

Sera couldn't pull herself away. Kya broke the silence between them.

"Are you really gonna sign yourself away like that?" she asked. "What's wrong with you?"

Sera moved out of Inaka's touch. "I truly apologize for how I've hurt you. This is a small price to pay to ensure your safety."

"Ouch," Inaka interjected. "I'm quite literally standing right here."

"But this doesn't make any sense," Kya shook her head. "How can I even trust that she'll keep her word?"

"*She* doesn't lie," Inaka said. "In fact, if you'll let me, I'd like to earn your trust."

Kya took a few steps back and looked up into Inaka's face, blue eyes narrowed. "All right, Carmilla. Prove it."

~ VII ~

OFFER YOUR BODIES AS A LIVING SACRIFICE

March 1818

Father Gōngzī Sera hadn't slept in days.

Her book of scriptures lay flat on the small wooden desk beside her bed. She tried going through it in order to find solace, but instead found that she could no longer make sense of what she was reading. Sentences jumped out of place, words she knew like the back of her hand suddenly unfamiliar. During Mass and other services, she had to be reminded of her duties frequently, duties she'd known since she was a child.

The raven haired woman she had met at confession continued to haunt her dreams. And while she was awake, the woman kept managing to find a way into the church. No matter how many guards were stationed at the doors, no matter who was warned to not permit her entry into the church, the woman consistently haunted her waking hours as well. Sera knew nothing about her - she always spoke very cryptically. She would show up when it was time for confession, demand Sera's time, *compliment her endlessly* and then leave. And in her dreams - oh, her dreams - the woman would appear out of nothingness. From within the void she would step into Sera's room through anything but its entrance; the windows, the fireplace, the mirror. Each time, she would keep her distance. She would recite poetry, read, or just sit in the windowsill as if she was perfectly content to keep watch over Sera as she drifted in and out of sleep.

May
Her family released her from duty, certain she was afflicted by some sort of sickness, a mysterious portent of things to come. No one else ever seemed to notice when the woman would come by. They were all beginning to wonder whether or not such a woman had ever even existed in the first place. She always wore fashions that Sera didn't typically see on the women in the area - low necklines, bodices cut end to end under the bust, shorter skirts. She would somehow silence Sera whenever she appeared in her room with nothing more than a finger pressed against her red covered lips.

June

She knew her family grew more and more concerned about her as the days passed. She heard whispers of calling in an exorcist, and Sera almost welcomed it. The woman had never laid a hand on her, and Sera couldn't tell if she was a hallucination or if she was something real. Her plans for her priesthood had been severely delayed and she wanted to be rid of this dark spirit plaguing her. She wanted to return to life as normal.

And yet, as the nightmares continued, Sera found that a seed was planted within her mind; some small and yet constantly growing sinful part of her began to crave the visits. It was a constant that she eventually came to rely on. Night after night, the woman would appear. She found herself desiring the smallest physical touch, even the light ghosting of their fingers against one another. She convinced herself that this was to ensure that the woman was, in fact, tangible rather than a figment of her imagination.

July

The lines between fiction and reality began to blur. Sera could no longer recognize whether she was awake or asleep. Instead of disappearing after a time, the woman stayed longer, lingered in the shadows of Sera's room longer, stalked in the corners of Sera's mind longer.

She saw the woman in her room in daylight, soaking up the rays of the sun. She approached slowly, a panther cornering her prey. There was nowhere else to run. The midday sun lowered in the sky behind her, illuminating the outline of her form while shrouding her in darkness. Sera trembled and pressed herself further back into her bed. She could just barely make out the features of her face in the concentrated darkness.

The woman held out her hand and said simply, "Come with me, and I shall share eternal glory with you."

Sera didn't have the mind to deny her.

She placed her hand in the woman's own and was immediately drawn closer against her. Her breath hitched in her throat, a jolt like lightning running down her body at finally having received that physical contact she so desperately ached for. The woman wrapped an arm around Sera's waist and held her tightly, fingers pressing against her hips in a possessive manner. Then, the world shifted in a cloud of smoke. Gone were the familiar wooden walls of Sera's room; once the smoke cleared and she regained her bearings, she found herself in the midst of cold, grey stone with indecipherable symbols and images painted against large tapestries. She figured they must be underground, that no sunlight would deign to reach this place. It was lit solely by an array of delicately placed candelabras, wax stalactites lengthening under spent candles.

The woman loosened her grip but did not let Sera go, walking her backwards. Her ears filled with the thrum of her heartbeat and the sound of her gasp once her legs touched plush velvet. Sera found herself on her back once more, with the woman perched on her lap. She gazed up into emerald eyes which seemed to blacken as she gazed down; the eye contact sent a fire into her stomach, a feeling she had never known before. And yet, somehow she knew such a feeling of such salaciousness was surely sinful.

What scared Sera was the fact that it didn't feel wrong.

In fact, she felt drawn like a month to a flame, a beggar to sustenance.

"Oh, my darling," the woman cooed, gently stroking her face.

The touch sent waves of sensation down the rest of her body, but it didn't quite penetrate the haze in her mind, the blurring of realities, and the intensity of the situation. Sera wondered if she could come down from this feeling, the sensations colliding to create such a cacophony that she wasn't sure how she stayed conscious. Her emotions swung wildly, like a pendulum.

The notion made her tense in bed. The woman above her felt her hesitance and frowned.

The pendulum swung again. It almost felt as if Sera's own body were diluting her instincts, calming herself down before she even knew she was panicking.

"Stay." The woman murmured a single word, softly grasping Sera's chin. "You're safe here, with me."

Even if Sera knew where *here* was, she wouldn't have contested. The woman made things sound so simple, so good. Stay. She didn't have to do anything but that. Sera wanted this, she realized. She wanted this more than she ever wanted anything in her life, possibly more than she wanted the approval and guidance of her god.

"Stay here and be mine," the woman continued, her hand moving from Sera's chin to her chest.

Sera took a few deep breaths and nodded; she wanted this.

"Be my pet, be right by my side. Let me own you and give you everything you've ever wanted from life," she cooed again.

"Own me?" Sera found her voice, however small.

If her eyes hadn't already blackened, Sera's quiet innocence sent the darkness into a new realm of oblivion, swallowed by obsidian and stretched far from any semblance of light.

"Yes, darling. I'll own you, you'll be all mine."

The pendulum swung.

Sera was waiting for the fear to enter her chest, some panic, apprehension. The only thing she felt was raw anticipation. Her words coiled around her extremities, traveled down deep inside of her, and did their bidding with Sera's body. She was a slave to feeling, on a high she had never before felt.

"I want that." "Please own me." "I don't want anyone to own me but you." Sera's claims, her staunch devotion, came rapid fire from her lips. She couldn't think; she was just feeling, letting the euphoria take over.

This attestation was all the woman needed. She lowered herself against Sera's body and pressed her lips against Sera's throat, then her shoulder blades, then the divot between them. Sera wasn't stupid - she knew what sex was. It was never meant to be for the devout priest that she had been in training to be. Somewhere in the back of her mind, she knew that if this continued, she would lose that part of her identity. And that same part of her wanted to find a new identity in how this nameless woman made her feel; in the way she tore open Sera's clothes and undergarments as if they were nothing more than tissue paper, in the way her hands pressed into her hips and forced her further down against the bed.

The woman sat back, gazing down at Sera in all her bare glory. If Sera could focus, she might have been self-conscious. But the desire and pure hunger in the woman's gaze made her very aware that she was a prized prey, something deliberately chosen for the explicit pleasure of her ravenous captor. And she was fine with that.

"You are as perfect as I imagined," she told Sera. She backed further down the bed and grabbed onto either of Sera's hips, angling her upwards. The mere touch of her fingers against Sera's bare skin nearly made her back arch off the bed. They felt smooth, so sure of themselves. She moved between Sera's legs and pressed her face between them, hands tightening. Her lips ghosted up the curve of Sera's thighs and then finally, blissfully, between her legs. Though her hands were holding so tightly Sera feared - and hoped - they might leave bruising behind, her tongue was gentle. She was tantalizingly slow at first, countering the writhing Sera couldn't seem to stop by digging her fingers into her hips further. Her eyes rolled back into her head and she could see stars exploding behind her eyelids. Her back did indeed arch and she moaned, surprising herself.

The woman's lips moved up Sera's pale thighs, slowly up her waist, tantalizingly up her torso. The woman opened her mouth and drew her tongue on the path from Sera's stomach up to the middle of her uncovered chest.

"Say that you are mine," she began, her voice a low growl, "forever."

"Forever," she repeated. Sera barely knew what she was agreeing to - if her agreement was even necessary - but she nodded eagerly. She felt the woman withdraw slightly, and opened her eyes to witness her biting down on her own wrist, and blood coated her lips once she pulled away.

Very quiet bells sounded in Sera's head, as if they were the far away ringing of her church's bells.

But the ringing of the alarms disappeared once the woman pressed her wrist to Sera's mouth.

"'This is the new covenant in my blood, which is poured out for you'," the woman quoted, a small smirk on her face. "'Drink of my blood and you shall have eternal life'."

And like any good servant kneeling at the altar, Sera obeyed.

It didn't have a taste beyond a strange, viscous thickness. Sera tried to pull away, but the woman kept her wrist pressed against Sera's mouth, her free hand wandering down between her legs. Sera's mouth opened in another involuntary moan, and she ended up swallowing more blood. Sera instinctively bucked her hips down onto the woman's fingers as she worked them, plunging deeper and deeper. Sera wanted to cry out, but the woman stopped her by crashing their mouths together in a bloody kiss. Sera could just barely taste herself on the woman's lips, on the tongue she shoved into her mouth. She could feel the tightness building up in her core, and felt herself tighten her legs against the woman's fingers.

And just as she was about to fall over the edge, the woman withdrew her fingers at a painfully quick speed and placed her hands on either side of Sera's head.

Her hands moved, roughly jerking Sera's neck to the side.

And everything went black.

And then everything came crashing back with a gasp. Her eyes still closed, she could hear more, taste more, *feel* more. Her resurrection sent her catapulting over the edge and she cried out in a voice that would shake the heavens, the arch in her back as she climaxed almost raising her off of the bed entirely. And instead of mere stars, she saw whole galaxies coming into existence as she did. As the blood in her veins turned into something different that turned her into *something different.*

She caught the breath she hadn't yet realized she didn't need, reaching up to touch the blood and tears mixing on her face.

And she awoke, born again.

~ VIII ~

LET NO ONE DECEIVE YOU WITH EMPTY WORDS

Coven Night continued to rage on. Inaka led them past bar after bar, past vampires leading humans and other creatures around by leashes or by sheer trained obedience. Here and there were groups of security werewolves, as stoic as their counterparts at the entrance to the event. If the scene bothered Sera, it downright outraged Kya. Inaka made Kya walk between her and Sera, with Nekiru and her human taking up the rear procession. Sera couldn't help but watch Kya go from looking around the event with disdain and disgust to staring pointedly at the back of Inaka's head. She imagined that Kya's curiosity had to be getting the best of her; Inaka hadn't compelled her, just promised something that would be worth her while. That had to be the only reason she was even still with them and hadn't tried to get away. Because if Sera had to compel her to get her here, there had to be a good reason she was staying with them of their own free will.

Was she...feeling jealous? Sera shook her head to clear the thought. There was nothing to be jealous of.

Inaka led them to a more permanent looking fixture, made with wood and pipes tensioned on a wide frame. Inaka halted the line and Nekiru came up from the back to open the door, letting them all filter in. Sera stopped short as the door closed behind her. The inside of the building somehow looked as if it was transported directly from Inaka's gothic castle; stone walls, leather tapestries, and a gilded throne at the back of the room. A large chandelier adorned with glistening black jewels and lit candles hung in the midst of the hall. Members of the Guàiwù bustled to and fro on orders long given, coven rings a deeper blood red under the light of the many candles. None of them paid any attention to the new entrants.

There was a wooden cabinet that came up to the arms of the lofty seat that Inaka moved to sit upon. She crossed her legs and opened it, searching through the levels.

"It's been a while since I've had the....pleasure of knowing a demon," she told them absently. "You meet one, you've essentially met them all."

Kya crossed her arms over her chest. "You're meant to be proving that I can trust you."

"I suppose you weren't made to be patient, were you?" Inaka asked. She arched a brow, but couldn't be bothered to give Kya her full attention.

Kya narrowed her eyes.

"Made from a dead human mage by Pario's angels, created for a specific purpose and let loose," Inaka continued. "No one really cares what happens to you after you fulfil your mission. You end up blending in with human societies, acting as their secret protectors until, one way or another, you die. Never having recovered the memories of your past."

"Are you going somewhere with this?" Sera asked.

Inaka pulled out a folded up parchment from the pile. "I would imagine that reclaiming those memories would be of great importance to a demon."

Kya straightened up immediately, her attitude gone. "You can do that?"

"I can certainly help. I've known some of the greatest human mages that ever existed. Killed a few of the original sixteen today's mages and demons are all descended from. It took them a couple centuries, but once they realized what the angels were doing with them when they died they tried to come up with ways to restore their memories. Not all of their tricks worked, and none of them worked consistently." Inaka held the parchment between two fingers and gestured with it as she winked. "Except for one."

Kya looked at Sera and smiled, hopefully. Sera smiled back, a small pang in her chest. Could this be what it took to get on Kya's good side? She wasn't even sure why she wanted to be on the demon's good side, but she knew that it was something she wanted more than anything in the world. But then Kya seemed to remember their circumstances, because her brows furrowed slightly and she turned away.

"This map tells you exactly where it's buried," Inaka said. "And it's yours, along with a full pardon against all past and future crimes against our kind. Provided my Sera plays her role perfectly."

All eyes fell upon Sera, who swallowed thickly and nodded. She knew what was expected of her. She had done it once before. It had been a big deal when Sera broke away from Inaka and went covenless. It was a hard few decades where she had to avoid supernatural creatures altogether. Whenever one came across her and eventually realized who she was, it always escalated to a life or death situation. She had killed enough of her kin and forced herself to subsist on enough of their blood that it weighed heavily on what was left of her conscience.

Inaka beckoned Sera forward with the crook of a finger. Realistically, Sera knew what happened to vampires who caught the attention of The Organization by remaining covenless for too long. She knew that she had no other choice. She knew she had agreed to do this, had agreed to go back into the fold, but her legs ached with finality every step of the way. If it meant Kya could be safe and happy, she would do it.

Sera bent down on both knees. Inaka pulled a dagger out from its sheath somewhere on her person and handed it down to her. She held the curved iron hilt in her right hand and pressed the blade against her left hand. She dropped her gaze, wincing as the holy water anointed blade bit into her skin. She dragged it across her palm as she spoke, smoke billowing out from the wound that would take weeks to heal.

"I, Gōngzī Sera, swear to you, Sato Inaka, that from this hour I will above all else be faithful to you. My actions will never bring harm to you. I will be part of your Guàiwù who my family are henceforth. I am voluntarily bound in the name of the sleeping god Mortem, who gives us all eternal life in her blood."

The hall was quiet. Sera's blood thundered against her ears as droplets dripped against the stone floor. She kept her head down, as was custom, waiting for Inaka to acknowledge her. And she did so by placing a high heeled foot under Sera's chin, tilting her head back.

"I've missed you dearly, Sera," Inaka said, her voice full of warmth. Sera could see tears in her green eyes, a pair that echoed her own. "Now rise."

Obediently, Sera got to her feet. Inaka took her wounded hand and slid a ring onto her finger, accepting her into the coven. Sera immediately looked at Kya; the look on her face said that this was the most horrid exchange she had witnessed yet, and Sera couldn't help but wince.

"I don't think I'll ever understand you," Kya said, her voice quiet.

"I don't think you'll ever believe me," Sera began, "but I want you to be happy."

"At your own expense? Were you always this self-sacrificing?"

"I was cast aside by my own parents like I meant nothing to them. Sacrifice is all I know."

Kya took a step towards her. "Don't think this one act changes how I feel about you. But...thank you. And if you wouldn't mind coming with me to retrieve this just in case Elizabeth Báthory sends her goons after me, I would appreciate the backup. We can split up after."

Sera nodded, biting down on her lower lip. She didn't expect Kya to suddenly care about her. She fully anticipated waking up in a few years or centuries on the wrong end of a weapon Kya would be wielding. Kya would most certainly be her undoing. She wasn't sure why that thought - that irrefutable fact - didn't frighten her. It was completely inexplicable, but if anyone had to do it, she wouldn't be so mad if it was Kya.

"Oh," Inaka said. Gone was all the warmth that had layered her voice just moments earlier. "Now this is a surprise."

"What is?" Sera asked, tilting her head.

"You *care* for the demon," Inaka said, accusingly.

Kya looked between the two of them, eyes wide as she took a few steps away. "What?!"

"Oh, you absolute hopeless romantic." Inaka laughed, though the sound was completely devoid of all humour.

Sera shook her head and raised her hands. "I don't know what you're talking about. I don't-"

Inaka got to her feet and closed the distance between them. She normally towered over Sera, her stature made even more impressive and terrifying with several inches of heels. "You offer yourself to me, you plead a case for this corpse, and she still doesn't want you. She can barely stand to look at you."

Sera's words were stopped by the new thickness in her throat and came out as a choked sob, a truly pathetic sound. If she had a heartbeat, it would be racing.

"Allow me to teach you a lesson, Sera," Inaka whispered.

She appeared at Kya's side and grabbed her chin, nails digging into her face. She gazed into her eyes, a strong, compelling voice when she spoke. "Offer yourself to me."

Immediately, Kya tilted her head to the side and moved her hair away from her neck. Inaka made sure to make eye contact with Sera, who was frozen in place, as she bared her fangs. Sera could only watch in horror as Inaka slowly bit down into Kya's tan flesh, and dark blood spurted out from the wound in response. Inaka drank and drank, forcing down the black blood until Kya began to waver on her feet in her weakened state. The inky blackness coated Inaka's lips as she pulled away, gripping tightly onto Kya's arms. She spit out what she could, making a disgusted face. She walked Kya backwards, her head lolling with the movement, and shoved her against Sera, who whimpered at the contact.

"No one will love you like I do, Sera," Inaka said with a low growl.

Kya, still barely conscious, tried to stand up on her own feet. Inaka pressed a bloody kiss to her forehead and said, "Don't remember this when you wake up, little demon." She took Sera's unblemished hand and pressed the parchment into it, then turned away without another word.

~ IX ~

A LIGHT UNTO MY PATH

1871

*Prior to leaving with Inaka that fateful night, Sera had never left her state. After her parents had abandoned her at the Gōngzī church, the building and its grounds were all she knew. She was schooled in the church's multipurpose building, with its permanent draft and **non-permanent** structure. She lived in its dormitory, wooden walls and rooms that looked exactly the same no matter the priestly rank. She helped take care of its farm, finding exercise and sanity in the routine that only changed with the seasons.*

After leaving with Inaka, it had taken her a while to understand what she was, what they were. Inaka, in her benevolence, had taken the time to fully explain that the world wasn't quite the narrow view that humanity had of it. Gone were the days of routine, of only knowing the church grounds. Humans shared the world with vampires, shapeshifters, fairies, and demons, though that had not always been the case. Prior to some apocalyptic event, they each had their own realm, each with their own gods – who in turn each had their own legion of angels - that had since been asleep. Vampires had Mortem, the god of death. Shapeshifters had Profectus, the god of change. Fairies had Fastus, the god of pride. Demons had Passio, the god of passion. And humans had Pario, the creator god. The one Sera had spent years worshiping and praising. The god who would no longer listen to her, because she was no longer his.

She didn't belong to the death god either, she knew that. She belonged to someone who - despite her awesome presence and beautifully calculating mind - somehow wasn't a god, though Sera and the rest of the coven worshiped her like one. Inaka made forever feel like a day. They didn't need to sleep, and so they didn't; during the day, they would retreat to their underground home and keep the party going there with whatever treasures they brought back. The coven existed for Inaka's magnificence and pleasure, and she shared all that she had built with her most faithful. To them, she entrusted matters of the utmost importance. At her direction, her disciples carried out atrocities in her name. Wherever they went, blood followed. They were strong. They were eternal. They were sacred.

Sera had never seen so much of the world. They couldn't stay in one place too long, lest the humans catch on to who and what they were.

It was only a matter of time before they made it back to Sera's home state.

Like a moth drawn to the flame, she was drawn back to her old life. She found her childhood home, its location dragged up from the depths of her memory by instinct and reflexes. A new family occupied the farm, but some part of Sera's brain saw them as the family she should have had. That stray thought was all that the creature of impulse that she was needed to tear the entire family apart, a merciless slaughter no amount of begging could end. Her rage carried her to the Gōngzī church mere hours before sunrise where she laid waste to the unfortunate clergy within, the last look on their faces being that of recognition and horror.

No longer did Sera bring promises of salvation and security for those who struggled. Now, she only brought death.

***

Sera couldn't let anyone see her cry.

She slid the parchment into her pocket and brought Kya up into her arms. She didn't look back at Inaka, keeping her head held high as she exited back out into the menagerie. They needed a space for Kya to recover before they made their next move. Having a task to focus on kept the tears at bay.

Sera ducked into one of the fixtures that functioned as makeshift hotel rooms, with beds and a lamp in every room. Ignoring the pointed smirks of the others in the large tent, she found a sectioned off room that had two twin beds. They probably assumed the worst, that she was here for the reason everyone else came into a space like this. But she merely laid Kya down on one of the beds and pushed the other to the complete opposite side of the room. She didn't bother to draw that binding symbol under Kya's bed as she had days ago in the church – if Kya attacked her here, she deserved it for what she'd let happen to her.

They probably should take the time to figure out what their best course of action was. If the parchment Inaka gave them led to some coveted treasure, it wouldn't be easy to access. The human mages were always said to be clever and clever people wouldn't leave important things unguarded. Even with all their strength and speed, a true and permanent death was still something to fear. Kya could be killed easier than Sera could, but they both could still meet their undoing if the path was as treacherous as Sera imagined it to be. Yet, they were alone in this world, buoyed only by each other. How could they find allies that they could trust?

"Knock, knock," someone said from outside of the room. Sera looked up to see Nekiru – and her human, of course – entering the room with an apologetic expression on her face. She was carrying Sera's small suitcase and a thick envelope in either of her hands.

"I'm sure you're not surprised that I'm here on behalf of Inaka," Nekiru began. She set down the suitcase and balanced the envelope on top of it. "You know how she gets when it comes to you. She knows it, too. She wants to apologize for hurting your companion and the pain it caused you."

Sera dropped her gaze.

"The two of you shouldn't go alone," Nekiru continued. "Inaka's sending people she trusts to help you. She doesn't expect you to forgive her immediately, but she wants you to know that she cares about you."

"What if I don't want her help?" Sera asked quietly, looking down at the wound on the palm of her hand. She flexed her fingers, head tilting at the strange sensation of pain.

"Unfortunately, you aren't allowed to decline her offer."

Sera let out a breath and nodded, closing her hand into a small fist.

Nekiru tapped her suitcase with her foot, sending it sliding along the ground over to Sera, who looked up. "I must say, it was nice to finally meet you." Nekiru told her, turning to leave. "I've been with her for thirty years, and she's talked about you every single day."

Inaka's assistant left then and Sera waited until she was sure the woman was out of earshot before shoving the parchment in her pocket and pressing her hands tightly over her face, blocking out the light coming from the lamp. Even if what Inaka said was true, even if Sera did have feelings for Kya, it wouldn't mean anything. Not only would Kya never reciprocate, Inaka could forbid them from interacting ever again. For Inaka to have lost control and acted out in anger like that, the idea of Sera being with someone else must have truly gotten under her skin.

Sera hadn't gone into this blindly. She knew what she was in for. She wouldn't have done anything different if it meant that Kya got what she wanted. When they parted ways, she would have to return to Inaka's side. She knew that the longer she stayed away from Inaka, she would steadily feel worse until the pain made her feel like a stake through the chest was the only option. Breaking away from the coven nearly killed her the first time; she knew she couldn't put herself through that pain again.

Sera shook the thoughts from her head and let out a breath. She reached down to grab the envelope on top of her suitcase. She could smell what it was before opening it – money, and lots of it. There was a small note on the inside, written in the hasty script of Inaka's cursive.

Give these fifteen thousand yuans to your demon when the time comes. She'll be able to start her new life or go back to her old one with comfort. I am already ashamed of my actions. I do hope you will be able to forgive me.

She could almost hear Inaka's voice in her head, reading the words aloud. If Kya didn't reciprocate the feelings Sera wasn't sure she even had, she could fall in love with Inaka again. She could let Inaka mold her into what she wanted and spend forever by her side. She could follow her to the ends of the earth, as she had for a century. As long as Kya was safe, Sera could be okay with never seeing her again. There were worse fates to suffer than being desired by a powerful, beautiful woman.

Sera slid the note in her pocket and laid her suitcase down to open it. Her pocket wasn't big enough to safely keep the envelope of yuans. When she opened the suitcase, her eyes widened. The envelope of money fell on the bed.

Neatly packaged on top of her things were rows of fresh blood. The humans had very recently invented the process of vacuum sealing things, and that made stealing and storing blood from hospitals quite a bit easier. It also kept the blood fresh longer, kept in the smell, and Sera had hopes that this present could last her the entire duration of their trip. She nearly lunged for one of the red-filled plastic and brought it to her mouth in relief. She hadn't fed since that night in the church, and it was beginning to take its toll on her. She could only hope that this blood had been offered willingly, and that whoever it came from was still alive.

Once Sera drank the bag dry, she let the crumpled plastic fall to the ground and licked her lips. She closed her eyes and felt instant relief, the pressing ache in her chest receding into something much more faint. Since she had left Inaka the first time, every drop of blood she'd had had tasted like guilt. She either felt guilty for killing a human, guilty for stealing from the hospital, or guilty and disgusted with herself for drinking the blood of a Guàiwù Inaka had sent to bring her back into the fold. But this was gifted to her.

She suddenly saw the allure of having a human pet as Nekiru did.

"You missed a spot, Dracula," Kya's voice groaned out, sitting up in the bed.

Sera opened her eyes to see Kya sitting up, stretching. She used the back of her hand to wipe at her mouth.

"What happened?" Kya rolled her shoulders. "Weren't we supposed to be following your ex? How did we end up in here?"

Sera knew she had to lie, as much as it pained her to. "You passed out. I haven't been doing a good job of making sure you eat when you're meant to."

Kya nodded slowly. "I don't suppose there's nothing around here for me to eat?"

"Nothing you'd like," Sera tried to joke. "Though I've read that human blood could sustain a demon just as much as human food can."

"Just because we have the stomach for it doesn't mean it's something we do."

"Then we should get going, shouldn't we? We'll buy you some food when we can."

"Going? Going where?"

Sera fished the parchment out from her pocket and walked it over. "This is supposed to lead us to something that will bring back your human memories."

"No shit?" Kya asked, snatching the parchment from Sera's outstretched hand. She unfolded it carefully while Sera sat back down, piercing blue eyes roaming over the full map. "And she gave this to you just because you agreed to join her little club?"

Sera rubbed the back of her neck. "She's not the worst person to exist. She also gave me this to give to you." She grabbed the envelope of money and lobbed it over

"Holy shit," Kya said, looking through the stacks of bills. "What's this for?"

"It's for you," Sera shrugged. "To start a new life once you get your memory back."

Kya looked between Sera and the money. Sera could see her brows twitch as she pieced things together. She knew there was no doubt in Kya's mind, as in her own, that this money also was to ensure Kya got far away from Sera. Kya likely didn't need to know how possessive Inaka was to figure that out.

"Fine by me," Kya said. "What are we waiting for then?"

Before Sera could say anything, two men walked into their room and stood at the door. The scent of the forest came in with them. One of them, Sera recognized. He was from Inaka's coven, stocky with planed features, long, straight, reddish brown hair, and pale brown eyes.

Looking at the other person was almost like looking into a mirror, if that was something Sera could still do. He was taller than she was, had intense eyes somewhere between green and brown, and certainly didn't smell like he was any kin of hers, but had the same angular jaw and straight nose that she did; she hoped her eyebrows looked better than his. Their eyes locked, and she assumed her surprise was mimicked in his own widened eyes.

"I'm assuming Inaka sent you both?" Sera asked.

The vampire Sera recognized, Akosi, spoke up first with a sarcastic two finger salute. "At your service, prodigal vampire."

"What exactly did she send you for?" Kya asked, suspiciously, looking between Sera and the man who looked as if he could be her twin.

"The two of us are supposed to be your knights in shining armor," Akosi continued, holding out his hand towards Kya. "We're supposed to make sure you get where you're going safely. Sera and I already know each other, but I can't say I've ever met a demon before. You look normal."

Kya sneered. "Wish I could say the same for you, bloodsucker."

Akosi grinned and withdrew his hand. "Cool, glad we've already decided on our dynamic." He patted the other man at his side on the back. "And this humourless fellow is Mako."

"I'm not humourless," Mako grumbled, crossing his arms over his chest.

"And I'm guessing he's a shapeshifter?" Sera trailed off.

"Wolf," Mako supplied begrudgingly. "I was lucky enough to be chosen when your mistress asked mine for assistance."

"I thought we didn't like shapeshifters?" Kya arched a brow at Sera.

"We don't," Sera said. "But if this one was already here, then he's probably trustworthy."

"Dogs are typically very loyal," Akosi added, ruffling Mako's hair. "What say you, ladies? May we accompany you on your journey?"

Sera looked at Kya and shrugged. The decision would be hers. If they were charged with getting Kya to her goal, then they all had something in common. And if anything went wrong, they could make effective distractions.

"Fine by me," Kya said. "The more of us there are, the easier it'll be for me to escape any dangers we might encounter."

"That's the spirit," Akosi agreed with a grin.

~ X ~

HONEY AND MILK ARE UNDER YOUR TONGUE

Sera wasn't sure that she fully trusted Mako and Akosi, but she had to admit that they were efficient. They looked at Kya's map and within a matter of minutes had come up with a camping plan that required lighters, ropes, a compass, and all the other tools necessary to be able to camp out on the journey. The trek would take them three whole weeks.

They waited for their escorts at the entrance to the cave that housed Coven Night's antics. One of the other covens, the Lamashtu, prioritized blending in with humans. They invented different ways of achieving this goal, from sunscreen that allowed them to walk in the light for a time to mirrors that were made with aluminium rather than silver. Akosi and Mako had gone to talk them into offering up tents that could block out the sun so they wouldn't have to waste time by going from motel to motel hours before sunrise.

Kya allowed Sera to hold and search the map while they killed time. According to the map, their destination was yet another cave a thousand miles away on the other side of the continent in the Yītóng mountain range. The name rang a bell for some reason, and it took a minute for Sera to recall why. The gods had originally intended to keep separate all the beings that lived within the different realms, their angels the only ones blessed with the ability to travel throughout them. But a fairy managed to kill an angel, used its power to travel the different realms, and made a deal with sixteen humans who lusted for power. The rebirth of the human mages made the realms come crashing together into one big Cataclysm that threatened to destroy the very fabric of reality. When all the realms came crashing together, the Yītóng mountain range was formed by the colossal first impact. Whole civilizations in each realm were wiped out in the ensuing catastrophe. Each society had their own name for the event; vampires called it The Cataclysm, humans referred to it as the Bronze Age Collapse. The chaos lasted for nearly three centuries and ended only once the angels sacrificed nine hundred and ninety-nine of their own and made the gods fall asleep.

Sera shared this knowledge with Kya, folding the map back up and handing it over. She ignored the way the fire in the pit of her stomach flared when their fingers brushed against each other. "I don't think a single realm was ever meant to handle more than one god." Sera said as she tried to take a step away as inconspicuously as possible, thankful that she couldn't blush.

"Did your ex ever tell you what was in the demon realm before they started making us from dead mages?" Kya asked. "I know that our realm was completely wiped out and that Passio's angels took up the job, but no one knew what we were like before."

"If she ever told me, I don't remember," Sera shrugged.

Kya pocketed the map and huffed. "Our oh-so benevolent creators aren't very hands-on. My first memory is looking up into the face of the angel that created me, and then I was handed off to my mentor. I never got the chance to ask the angel what I was created to do."

"You don't know what your purpose is?"

"I have a purpose..." Sera swore she saw Kya's gaze flicker to her for the briefest of moments, "had a purpose. But I was never assigned anything. I was in training for decades, and was so focused on doing what was expected of me that it took me a while before I realized I couldn't connect with my past life."

"Decades? You don't look like you've even reached your thirties."

"Well, neither do you. No matter how I grow and change, I always look the same. I can't grow my hair out, have no need to cut my nails, and I'm sure you've noticed that I don't need to relieve myself ever."

"But you need to eat?"

Kya tilted her head. "Still need an energy source. If I don't eat a certain amount, I'm fairly certain I'd die within a day or two. For good this time."

Sera swore she could hear Inaka's voice in her head. *That's awfully complicated.* She shook her head, clearing her thoughts.

Akosi and Mako came into Sera's line of vision then, carrying supplies and a rolled up tent under each arm. They set them down at their feet and took stock of everything they had again, dividing everything up amongst the four of them.

"Don't you have something else you could wear?" Akosi asked, looking up at Sera from where he knelt.

Sera frowned and looked down at her outfit. She had been alternating between the same three cassocks she had left her church with. "What's wrong with what I'm wearing?"

"For starters," Mako began, "why are you pretending to be a human priest? You stand out."

"But I *am* a-" Sera cut herself off. With an ache in her heart, she realized that the man who had her face was right. She had lost her right to call herself a priest when she took Inaka's hand. Nothing she could do would erase her past, especially when juxtaposed against the inevitability of her future. Her destiny had always been this. It was probably only a matter of time before she had her hand in toppling human regimes yet again. The voice in her head reminded her that she was, as Mako said, merely pretending to be a priest. Pretending that she could regain the future she had thrown away, that she had anywhere to go but back to Inaka. Pretending to be human, pretending to offer a space for safety and security for the humans she pretended she could love on the site of her most cruel atrocity. She had been pretending for the past twenty years.

It was about time that she stopped.

With a quiet and angry grunt, Sera pulled the cassock over her head, revealing her white shirt and dress pants underneath. A part of her considered simply shoving it into her suitcase, but the dominant part of her crumpled it up marched to the lip of the cave and tossed the mass of fabric over the side. She leaned over and watched her old life fall away from her, staring until she could no longer distinguish the black of her old uniform from the black of the night.

Sera heard Akosi mumble behind her, "Well that seemed like an overreaction."

The first few days of the trip were uneventful. Sera eventually threw out her other cassock suits. Kya offered to buy her a new set of clothes, and that eventually turned into a group shopping trip at Akosi's behest. The boys had rather limited options, but Kya and Sera had their choice of dresses, shorts, pants, pantsuits, and accessories. Mako recommended that they try to blend in for the occasions when they stopped for food. Humans recently developed a vested interest in fast food, and none was more popular than a particular chain that prided itself on its fried chicken. They would stop there once or twice a day when they had the option to, as it was the fast food chain that Mako and Kya preferred to all the others. While vampires couldn't enjoy human food as deeply as others could, Kya and Mako's voracious inhalation of the offerings at that chain made Akosi and Sera feel as if they were missing out.

A week in, they wolfed down the food and the vampires managed to convince themselves that they enjoyed it.

"You don't have to use that term, you know," Mako complained when Sera tried to joke. "Wolves aren't that messy."

"Fuck, you really are humourless." Kya rolled her eyes.

"See!" Akosi exclaimed, looking vindicated. "I've known this dog all of one month and I don't think I've ever seen him smile."

"Maybe don't call him a dog," Sera suggested around a mouthful of food. "That sounds like a microaggression."

"Oh, it is," Akosi nodded. "But you should hear what he calls us when he thinks I can't hear him."

"What does he call you?" Kya asked with a grin. "Let me get out my notebook, I'm running out of names."

"Come on, man," Mako complained.

Akosi raised his hand and ticked off the names on his fingers. "Leech, oversized mosquito, drainer, cold-skin, sucker, fang-face, tick, long teeth-"

Sera almost completely doubled over as Akosi continued. Kya was slamming a fist against the table, laughing at the top of her lungs. Mako pointedly looked out the window, his cheeks heated in a blush. They drew the attention of the humans in the eatery but barely noticed. And for the first time in her whole life, Sera felt that getting along with the people around her was utterly and completely effortless.

And the voice in her head told her it wouldn't last.

Before each morning's sunrise, they would take the time to scout out a good camping location. Each night, they found the grouping of trees with the thickest leaves through which the sun's rays could barely pierce. Each night, they set up their sun blocking tents and waited out the day.

Sera had the same routine each day. She would open her suitcase and read one of the books she had brought with her. If she could no longer be a priest, she got it in her head that she could make a career in books and knowledge. She could open a supernatural library or explore the world – without merciless slaughter this time. She could see their world through something other than a blood-fueled haze. She could take in the beauty it had to offer her.

After reading, each night she would dig into one of her presents. It had been so long since she was this consistently fed, so long where the painful burn in her chest and throat were everyday occurrences. Her guilt disappeared, little by little, with each bag she consumed. The voice in her head told her that she could keep her hands clean *and* stay strong and fed – she could get a willing human pet, or she could rely on Inaka to keep getting her presents. She had felt weak for so long that feeling and keeping her strength felt great.

When she finished drinking, Sera would lean back on her sleeping bag and let the feeling of renewed strength wash over her. She could imagine the power running through her body, circling its way through her system. It would heal her, re-energize her, solidify her in this life. It would cleanse her from all her impurities and false idols. It would put a new spirit in her, washing away the guilt with a more euphoric feeling.

Her thoughts always wandered when this feeling came upon her; as did her hand, as if it had a mind of its own. She would close her eyes and let the dark shroud her as her fingers slipped beneath the waistband of her pants. Sometimes she would think of Inaka, sometimes of Kya. Sometimes both.

When she thought of Kya, of her dark skin and light eyes, of the taut muscles that covered her body, the vision in her head never spoke. The demon in her head looked up at her with a mixture of disgust and pure lust, as if they both knew they shouldn't be doing what they were doing but couldn't help themselves regardless. She would think of the looks Kya had given her during the day, convincing herself that the girl was doing the same thing in her own tent. Maybe in Kya's mind, she was being pinned down by Sera, being touched by her, being caressed by her, being seen by her.

When she thought of Inaka, of her ivory skin that was cold to the touch, of her long and slender legs, the vision in her head always spoke. She could always hear Inaka's voice. The vampire in her head looked down at her in awe, as if she was the most holy and sacred thing in Inaka's life. The Inaka in her head would place her lips by Sera's ear and recite the most scandalous of scripture as her long and slender fingers brought Sera's underwear to the side.

"You have captivated my heart, my bride," the voice in her head would say. "You have captivated my heart with one glance of your eyes." And when the slender fingers began to move their way inside, "How beautiful is your love, my bride. How much better is your love than wine, and the fragrance of your oils than any spice." And when red coated lips would be pressed to her own, "Your lips drip nectar, my bride; honey and milk are under your tongue." And when those lips would work their way down Sera's stomach, "A garden locked is my bride, a spring locked, a fountain sealed. Your shoots are an orchard of pomegranates with all choicest fruits, with all choice spices, a garden fountain, a well of living water."

And Sera would respond, "Let my beloved come to her garden, and eat its choicest fruits." And Inaka would indulge herself.

And Sera would ride out the euphoria, grasping onto it with both hands until it ushered her into sleep before any of the guilt returned.

Mako would always be the one to wake them up when the sun had set sufficiently. They didn't speak to each other while they packed their things and got ready to run again, needing time to remember that they all, to some extent, enjoyed each other's company as much as one could enjoy the company of people they were stuck with. As usual, they looked for their food as soon as they got close to a bigger human city. And as usual the closest city had an assortment of fast food places to choose from but their group only had eyes for one.

But as soon as they pushed open the doors they were hit with a fresh wave of the forest scent. They had become accustomed to it as shapeshifters hid amongst humans often, but it was always a terse moment. The shapeshifters they encountered always looked like a flight risk, ready to either run or attack them at the first sign of danger. And a part of the whole "laying low" thing they were trying to do among humans meant they couldn't let that happen. Sera glanced back at Mako, who was already searching the nearly empty restaurant, subtly trying to sniff out the source. He made his way to the counter and rang the bell, and a familiar face came to greet them.

"Welcome to –" the girl from the motel began, then cut herself off abruptly when she looked up into their faces. "Oh, it's you."

"You're lucky I'm in the mood to eat and not fight," Kya told her, crossing her arms over her chest. "I expect that we'll get this meal for free, all things considering."

"You guys know her?" Mako asked, tilting his head.

"She took all our money before we made it to the event, if that counts as knowing her." Sera provided with a shrug of her shoulders.

"That was in the past," the girl said with a grin. "I've been hoping to run into you again. Stayed in one place, assuming you'd eventually come here."

"Why, so you could apologize?" Kya asked with a scoff. "Do you know how hard it is to find food without money? You could've killed me."

"I wanted to make it up to you, honestly," she replied. "Look, order and have a seat. I'll go on break and tell you more."

"Why should we believe anything you have to say?" Sera asked. "We don't even know who you are."

"Well that's an easy fix," the girl said with a laugh. "My name's Beak."

~ XI ~

I CREATE LIGHT...

They ate their meal – on the house – and waited for Beak to get on her break. Sera kept an eye on her while the others ate, just in case the girl tried to run out the back. But she kept her word and when she made it through the dinner rush, she nodded at them to guide them outside to the back of the building.

"What made you so sure that you'd run into us again?" Kya asked, arching a brow.

"Small world, ain't it? When we talked, you let it slip that this joint was your favourite place to eat. So I applied." Beak drew out a pack of luckies from her back pocket and tapped a flat palm against the bottom of the package before freeing a single cigarette from its case. "It was only after our little run in that I heard that the vampire covens are plotting to do something big. Fucked up and big. I was hoping to run into you and the priest at some point."

"You think they have something to do with it?" Mako asked, frowning.

Akosi jerked his head towards Mako. "We already have one of your kind on our little team. Do you not trust him?"

"First of all, he's not one of *my* kind." Beak placed a cigarette between her lips. She snapped her fingers in front of the opposite end, and a flame jumped from her fingers to light it.

"Ah, you're a Phoenix." Sera knew the basics about shapeshifters. She knew that there were about five-thousand different types, all mammals and birds. Each type had their own rules and groups, and she wouldn't be surprised if they didn't get along well with each other. Unlike vampires, they had no central organization or government, and mostly lived in forests. They didn't typically spend their time trying to blend in with humans.

Beak took a long drag and then blew out the smoke, winking at Sera. "Got it in one."

Kya cleared her throat and crossed her arms over her chest. "What does their plan have to do with us?"

"And can we replace Mako with you?" Akosi raised his hand. "I assume you can't die, right? That'll make our little group a lot more formidable."

"I mean, I can die. I'd just come back an hour or so later," Beak said with a shrug. "Some pure iron to the chest would kill any of us."

"Can we get back to the topic at hand?" Kya growled out. "What are they planning, and what does it have to do with us?"

Beak blew out a cloud of smoke and pointed to Sera and Akosi, both of whom took an offended step back. "Why don't you ask them?"

"Okay, clearly you've got something wrong," Akosi laughed. "We're all doing something for," he gestured at Kya, "the demon. We're going to help her get her memory back."

"Maybe you could just tell us what you think is going on?" Mako asked.

Beak tilted her head back against the building. "The vampires are planning to wake the gods."

The collective began to speak at once, voicing their concerns. Beak raised a hand to quiet them.

"Vampires like to talk, so you've just got to make them know you'll listen," she told them.

"How is this even supposed to happen?" Sera asked, taking a step forward. "If they wake the gods, if it's even possible, that could cause another Cataclysm."

"Well, darling, if I knew how it would happen, would I be here?"

"Can we stop wasting time?" Kya threw her hands up, looking at the rest of the group. "Whoever this person is, she's making us lose time. Let's go."

The others lifted their shoulders in shrugs, and Sera was inclined to agree. Try as they might, the vampires couldn't possibly wake all the gods. The only ones who could probably even hope to do that were the remaining angels, and Sera couldn't see them doing something that stupid any time soon. Sera made a mental note to ask Inaka about such a claim when she returned from Kya's journey.

The group turned to leave, grabbing their camping gear from the ground. A wall of fire went up in front of them. Beak walked through the fire, wings of flame spreading out four feet in either direction. Her green eyes reflected the fire as it flickered and died down.

"You aren't going anywhere," Beak began with a smile, "without me." She pointed her dwindling cigarette at Sera. "The priest and I can share a tent."

"Like fuck you will," Kya growled out. "If you insist on coming, you carry your own weight. You can find yourself your own tent or sleep on the floor, I don't care."

And Beak did insist on joining them for the rest of their trip. When they stopped to rest, she would fly herself up above the tops of the trees and extinguish her wings, then drop into the thicket. Her presence didn't really seem to bother anyone but Kya, even when she used her employee discount to get them free food. Everyone but Kya became accustomed to her presence. So accustomed, in fact, that Sera had caught her coming out of Mako and Akosi's tents on multiple occasions – and Sera would be lying to herself if she claimed that she hadn't thought about it, that there wasn't a new face she thought of during the day.

Kya would complain that the trip had suddenly gotten so much worse and so much more arduous, or that Beak slowed them down. The worst part of the trip, in Sera's opinion, was setting up the tents. She had no idea if they were always so complex or if their added complexity was due to the Lamashtu's adjustments, but it was the only thing that got her angry during their travels. With a day left into their trip, the landscape had changed – there were less trees and the ground under their feet became harder and rockier. Coupled with the knowledge that she and Kya would be parting ways, Sera's impatient anger managed to snap one of the flimsy tent poles. And then another. After the third one snapped, she clenched her fists and walked far into the sparse forest to try to calm down.

It wasn't long before she heard some footsteps coming up behind her.

"Whoever it is, please just give me space," Sera said with a groan. She combed her fingers through her hair and shook her head. "I'll be back to camp soon."

"It's me," Kya's voice said, forcing Sera to spin around at the sound.

They made eye contact. Sera's mouth opened and closed. In just a short amount of time they would have to part ways. Kya had been a part of Sera's life only for several months, and yet she had a hard time imagining what the future would look like without her. But it would be selfish of her to ask her to stay. She would have to go back to Inaka, and Inaka would never let Kya stick around. And Sera feared she wouldn't survive severing their coven link again, especially when she knew the pain that would await her if she tried.

"I need to know something," Kya told her, rubbing the back of her neck as she gazed at the ground.

"Anything," Sera replied, almost breathlessly. Why did she look so shy? Was Kya thinking the same thing? Was she about to admit that when she laid in her tent sleeping the day away, she dreamed of Sera? Would she confess that sometimes her hand would wander as Sera's own did?

"Why did you lie to me?" Kya asked instead, forcing Sera out of her own head.

"W-what? When did I lie to you?"

Kya looked up then, and Sera saw that she wasn't shy at all – she was furious. Her jaw was clenched tightly, her breathing shallow, and Sera swore she could see some patches of demon red overtaking her deep brown skin. "You think I didn't know that you lied to me before we left Coven Night? I wouldn't pass out if I didn't get enough to eat in a day– I would *die*. I gave you the chance to tell me the truth."

If it had been doing anything, Sera's heart would have stopped then and there.

Kya strode forward, shoving flat palms against Sera's chest and forcing her backwards. "You made me think you had changed, that you were capable of changing!"

"But I am!" Sera pleaded as she stumbled back. "I have! How I feel about my past is no secret!"

"You think that just feeling bad about what you've done absolves you of your sins?" Kya yelled, tears in her eyes. "You were a killer for a century! You haven't even *begun* to atone for what you've done!"

"I want to be better. You know that. You made me remember what it was like to feel something instead of going along with the motions." Sera winced as she spoke, but found that she didn't regret it once she said it. She ignored the voice in her head telling her that this was a mistake. "Mako was right, I was pretending for so long. I don't know how much longer I would have gone on pretending, gone on without actually feeling anything, but you saved me from that."

Kya searched Sera's eyes for a while and balled up her fists. She hit them against her chest again, but there was no force behind it. Sera took the assault anyway. "I need to know what happened, Sera."

Sera took a deep breath. "You asked me to come with you, to help you get here. And Inaka...didn't take it all too well. She bit you and compelled you to forget it ever happened."

Kya's brows furrowed as she looked up into Sera's eyes. "Why would she do that? I know for a fact that demon blood is repulsive to vampires. It's not like she could have killed me that way."

"She wanted to teach me a lesson."

"Why would teaching you a lesson mean she had to hurt me?"

"She was upset. She said that I cared for you. More than she was comfortable with."

"And do you?" Kya asked quietly. "Do you care for me?"

Very quiet bells sounded in Sera's head, as if they were the far away ringing of her former church's bells. She looked down into Kya's eyes and searched them, for any sign as to how her next words would be taken.

And she couldn't find the words.

Sera instead leaned down and crashed their lips together. Kya hesitated for the briefest of moments before she grabbed onto Sera's shirt and pulled their bodies flush against each other. Sera kissed her like she was the sun, like she was something worth dying for. Kya pushed back just as hungrily, and when Sera wrapped an arm around Kya's waist to pull her body even closer, Kya rewarded her with a breathy moan. She could feel the heat rise in Kya's cheeks and the warmth was enough to nearly force her out of her body. But she made herself stay present, to drink in the sensation of Kya's tongue pushing its way past her lips. For this moment, the voice in her head quieted. She could worry about the repercussions later. All she could focus on was the way Kya's lips felt against hers, the way their hands roamed across each other's bodies with unbridled passion. Kya slipped a hand under her shirt and Sera slid a hand in her short hair.

Kya pulled back slightly, keeping her body pressed against Sera's own. She panted, her chest heaving with the motion. "When is a monster not a monster?" she mumbled.

Sera didn't have a response. She was monster, she knew that. But perhaps she was a monster capable of being loved into something better.

"What do we do now?" Sera whispered.

"I don't know," Kya admitted.

"My tent is broken."

Kya coughed out a laugh, and Sera was certain it was the most precious sound she had ever heard. She would give anything to hear it for the rest of her life.

"You can stay in mine. I'll sleep outside. The sun won't hurt me." Kya said with a sigh.

Sera pressed their lips together again. They shared a kiss far more gentle this time, like light rain on a summer evening. Kya melted against her, fitting perfectly against her body.

They returned to camp just in time, and Sera dove into Kya's tent. It took her some time to fall asleep – when she woke up, they would ascend the mountain, find what they had been looking for, and restore Kya's past life. Whatever came next would be dealt with when the next night came.

Which it did, abruptly.

When Sera woke up, she was no longer inside of Kya's tent. She wasn't sure what she was looking at, how to make sense of the scene before her. There was a large black and grey wolf chained to a tree, snarling and lunging. There was an incinerated corpse with an iron rod sticking through its chest, the foliage around it reduced to ash. Another body lay face down, twitching, with an assortment of ancient looking bottle littered around their head. Sera tried to move, to figure out what was going on, but found that she couldn't move. She realized that she was viewing all of it from an strange angle, as if she was laying on her side. And then the view shifted; she was moving, though she wasn't doing the action herself. She tried to move her arms and felt them burn and smoke rise as soon as she did. The same happened when she tried to move her legs. Sera cried out as ropes laced with holy water bit into her skin.

"Help!" she yelled. Where was Kya? Where were the others? Where was *she*? "Kya? Kya, where are you?"

The movement stopped suddenly, and she fell flat on her back. She realized she was tied to a piece of wood, her arms outstretched and her legs together. The next voice that spoke surprised her just as much as the words the voice said.

Akosi walked into her line of vision. He crouched down to kneel next to her. "Don't worry about your friend. Inaka keeps her word."

"Inaka?" Sera asked groggily.

"While you two were busy, I got that weird memory potion that you were after," Akosi continued as if she hadn't spoken. "Brought it back, made her drink it. Dealt with the others. They should be fine, but I can't say I care too much either way."

"What?" Sera asked again. She bit down on her lip, trying to keep from crying out at the pain.

"You should have seen this coming, really," Akosi told her with a sigh. He pushed himself back to his feet and walked away. "But don't worry, she'll explain everything soon."

Sera began moving again as Akosi dragged her up the Yītóng mountain.

~ XII ~

...AND CREATE DARKNESS

The pain forced Sera to drift in and out of consciousness.

When she was awake, she hallucinated as Akosi dragged her up the mountain's incline. Sometimes she heard wolves howling. Once, she thought she saw the expanse below her explode into flames. Another instance had the whole valley light up in a great, white, light.

The next time Sera opened her eyes, she was in complete darkness. Too dark for her to make sense of. A shift let her know that she was still outstretched and tied down to the dogwood. Even though she had been drinking blood bags on a nightly basis, she wasn't strong enough to break free from her bindings. Even the slightest strain against the ropes would make the burn return, sapping her strength. She knew that fighting was useless. Whatever happened next would happen no matter how she felt about it.

What *would* happen next? Why did Akosi bring her here? She knew that he had dragged her up the Yītóng mountain and that Inaka had a part to play in this. Was it because she and Kya had kissed? Had Inaka somehow known this would happen? Did Akosi see them when it happened? She wanted to fault him for doing this to her, but he was just following orders that he couldn't disobey. And she couldn't fault Inaka for it, either. Not that she didn't want to.

Sera couldn't tell how long she laid there in the dark. It could have been an hour. It could have been longer; the way the ache in her throat returned let her know that it was likely the latter. Her limbs began to feel stiff from disuse, and on occasion she would wonder if she had been left to simply rot in the cave. She wasn't entirely sure what would happen if she were to remain still for an exorbitant amount of time. When she went without blood, being around blood was what drove her thirst. But it felt as if she was entirely alone in the dark, the only smell being her own, the only sound the faint echo of a steady drip of water. Could she die if she didn't drink? She had never heard of it in all of the history of her kind, but that didn't mean it was completely impossible.

She was certain that time passed, and it tested her theory the more it stretched on. The ache in her throat didn't get any more pressing than how it felt when it first appeared. With naught else to think of, her mind explored different realms of possibilities. Why did they need to drink blood, anyway? They didn't need to breathe or sleep – though they could do those things – and they could eat human food, though it didn't taste like anything more than flavoured cardboard. Did the vampires who existed before The Cataclysm live off of blood? Where was that source before humans crashed into their world? If blood was an energy source, could Sera die from going without it? How long would it take?

She occasionally heard Inaka's voice in her head. Sometimes they had whole conversations, and sometimes Inaka would speak to her in a language that Sera didn't know. Human vampire hunters had a penchant for Latin – though it had stopped being a lingua franca after the Third Century Crisis – so most vampires knew it, but it certainly wasn't what Sera's hallucination of her mistress would use to talk to her. She wondered if it was one of the languages The Organization used, Enochian or Nephilim, to ensure that their already cryptic messages were decidedly more cryptic.

For the most part, Sera wasn't too concerned about not feeding. If she was kept locked up like this, she wouldn't hurt anyone; she couldn't be tempted by blood that she couldn't access. But that feeling changed once she began to feel tired. It terrified her, one of the few sensations she hadn't encountered since she was human. Her body was convincing her brain that it needed to sleep, which probably meant that it was shutting down and wanted to spend whatever energy it had left on delaying that shut down for as long as possible. When this started, Sera did whatever she could to stay awake.

She thought about all the death and destruction she had caused when the world fell to its knees before her. She thought of never questioning why she was sent to kill someone, of why she found that divine warmth she had sorely desired under a mountain of death. The voice in her head told her that there was a purpose, that all that death and destruction made her stronger. But, tied down to a carving of wood, she didn't feel all that strong.

If the vampires raised the gods, like the shapeshifter claimed they wanted to, would any of them accept Sera? What would she do to find and keep the love she desired? And if all she wanted was love, why had she stayed away from someone who had only ever wanted to love her?

She couldn't help but think about Kya. She knew Kya wouldn't come for her, especially now that she had her memories back. It was easier this way, with Kya off reconciling with her past life and Sera far, far away from her. They were going to have to part ways regardless. This way, neither of them would have to feel any guilt, and Sera wouldn't have to sever her coven link.

Her coven link.

She was in a whole new universe of pain, but none of it was the specific gut-wrenching, rib-crushing, spine-stabbing pain that came with severing a coven link. Inaka had to be nearby. Likely however long she had been here, tied down in the dark.

It took Sera a while before she could convince her vocal cords to work again.

"Where are you?" She croaked out. "I know you can hear me, Inaka. Where are you?"

Eventually Inaka responded in her head. *I've been with you this whole time, my beloved. You don't need to fear.* Sera had never been hallucinating. The voice in Sera's head had been hers this whole time.

"No- don't pull this with me," Sera yelled back. "I know you're here. Physically here. Or at least you're close enough to get here quickly."

You don't need to yell.

"And you didn't need to do all of this. I would have willingly come here with you."

I know that now. But I worried she would turn you against me, and I need you.

"You owe me, Inaka. You owe me the truth, after all that I've done for you. You owe me freedom."

Inaka didn't respond to that. She didn't respond the next few times Sera tried to yell out to her. She strained against the ropes, even as they bit down into her skin and began smoking.

She fell back on old habits and ran through the scriptures in her head from end to end, seeking revelations that had yet to be discovered. She wasn't deluded into thinking that she had the right to still call herself a priest, but she found some comfort in the words that had been a source of solace for others long before she had existed. Maybe in another life, if she was so lucky, she would be able to experience the bliss of Pario's love. It had been so well documented in the scriptures that a younger, human Sera sought after it with all her heart. But he must have known what she would become, that she would end up here, because she had never once felt Pario's warmth.

She had never felt so utterly alone as she did in the dark. If her eyes were ever allowed to see the light again, she wasn't sure she could even handle it.

She didn't know if Inaka was putting the thoughts in her head or if this was her brain's own doing, but she reflected on the fun they had together. Sera knew there were good times in her past. The time she had spent with Inaka, especially the time where they weren't killing innocent humans, meant something to her. She had taken her in and saved her from mortality. Inaka had taught her about the realms and the gods and all the things humans were meant to learn that Sera had never gotten the chance to before her parents decided they no longer wanted her. Inaka had brought her to Greece, to Turkey, to Egypt, to the Maghreb. Together they watched as humanity went from horse drawn carriages to metal contraptions that used steam, then gasoline. They saw the apex of the Industrial Revolution and its effects around the world.

"Where are you?" Sera asked the empty nothingness. She wasn't sure who she was yelling for.

Did she want Kya to come and save her, like a damsel in distress? Did she want Inaka to set her free? Did she want the gods to prove that she was worthy of love after all?

In the end, it was Inaka who came to see her. Sera caught her scent long before she showed up; black roses, leather, dragon's blood. After so long with nothing to stimulate her senses, it was overwhelming and powerful. The scent was so familiar and warm that Sera could forget just how upset she was with Inaka. And when the woman herself showed up carrying an oil lamp, her beautiful face and adoring gaze was the first thing Sera saw emerge from the light.

This was what love smelled like.

This was what love looked like.

"I am sorry that it took so long for me to get here," she said, her voice dripping with honey. "I hope you will be able to forgive me."

This was what love sounded like.

She set the oil lamp down on whatever surface the wood was laying on and pulled thick gloves over her deceptively delicate fingers. She untied Sera's legs, bound at her ankles. The limbs felt like little more than dead weight, and Sera knew she wouldn't want to look at how raw her skin was. The spaces where the ropes touched her skin felt like they had been rubbed down to the bone, and she couldn't bear to see that. Instead, she looked up into Inaka's face.

"Oh, my beloved," Inaka whispered as the bundle on her right arm fell. "Soon this will be over."

"We're in the mountain?"

Inaka spoke, untying the rope on Sera's left arm. "Do you remember why this mountain is important?"

"It was the first place all the realms intersected," Sera replied.

The rope fell, and Sera was completely free. Inaka nodded as she gently pressed Sera's arms down against her side, her gentle touch offsetting the ache that came from keeping her arms in that position for so long.

This was what love felt like.

"Because of that, it's a place of immense power." Inaka massaged Sera's arms lightly, as if urging what was under her skin to begin working again. "It's the only place formed by all six realms."

"Six?" Sera asked. "You've always told me there was only five."

"Six, when you count the realm of the gods."

Inaka helped her to sit up. Sera tried to flex her muscles as feeling returned to her extremities painfully slow. She twisted and looked back at her prison, a stack of wood cut into the shape of a lowercase "t" atop a stone table.

"I didn't want to have to resort to such dramatics," Inaka told her. She placed a finger under Sera's chin and turned her head to make eye contact. "I couldn't risk losing you. You understand that don't you?"

Sera nodded. Inaka kissed her.

This was what love tasted like.

"I would have come to get you sooner, but that friend of yours kept me busy for a while," Inaka continued. "I wanted to be here as soon as Akosi dropped you off, but restoring her memories seems to have given her back some of her old magic. She and those two shapeshifters of hers have been relentless in trying to take you away from me again."

Kya came to rescue her?

Did she need rescuing?

"How long has it been?" Sera asked.

Inaka hesitated. "You must understand, Sera, I had planned to relocate you within days, maybe weeks. But because of her, and because I promised you that I wouldn't harm her, you've been here for six months. I can't imagine how thirsty you must be."

Sera hadn't felt thirsty since the first time she spoke to Inaka, but she knew she couldn't trust herself to be around anything with a pulse. If Inaka were anyone else, if her mistress wasn't someone she loved, Sera's hunger might have made a resurgence.

"Either way, I have a surprise for you," Inaka began. "I wanted to celebrate your return to me. But I will need you to trust me, as you did all those years ago when I first took you away. Do you still trust me?"

She held out her hand. Sera took it without hesitation.

"Always."

Inaka smiled down at her. Sera tried to move off the table, but found her legs wouldn't quite cooperate. She lurched forward and fell right into Inaka's welcome open arms. Without missing a beat, Inaka brought her up into her arms. She held onto Sera as if she was the most precious thing in the world, the rarest jewel fit for a royal.

"You're the most important thing in the realms to me," Inaka told her as she started to walk, careful not to jostle Sera's recovering body. "And I love you more than anything else. Because of that, what happens next will depend entirely on you."

"What do you need me to do?"

She carried Sera further up into the mountain, some light source making their path brighter and brighter. But Sera only had eyes for Inaka. "Only what you've been doing since we met. We've done incredible things together, my love. The prospect of eternity was boring until I met you. You made me feel, for lack of better terms, alive." Inaka laughed, and the sound echoed from her chest. "You never asked why I would send you on assignments to kill certain people here and there, and it's about time you found out."

The light became nearly blinding. Sera turned her head to finally face what her destiny. They were approaching a decadent room that looked too beautiful to have been created inside of the mountain. The room was lit by candles and glistening, multi-coloured jewels buried in the rock. The room's floor was completely made of white marble with repeating black patterns. Ivy wrapped around rows of white marble columns. Gold banners decorated the singular long, rectangular table in the midst of the room and gold tapestries decorated the walls. There were eleven masked guests sitting at the tables in black suits and dresses. It was the picture of opulence.

And all Sera could think about was the blood.

There must have been a slaughter, because there was a large symbol drawn in blood in the midst of the beautiful marble floor. A statue with its back facing them rose from the middle of it, its rocky, misshapen base looking as if it had come forth from the depths of the mountain itself. Blood filled the goblets and the dishes. The only thing stopping Sera from launching herself forward out of Inaka's arms and licking the tantalizing stuff from the floor was the fact that she still had not regained full control of her body. Inaka held on to her tightly to keep her from falling flat on her face.

"It's almost time for that, darling," Inaka told her. Sera could hear the pride in Inaka's voice, and it was almost as tempting as the blood.

She involuntarily twitched in Inaka's arms as they strode into the room, so overwhelmed by the red that it was all she could see. Her vision turned red, and she imagined herself drinking the world dry. It turned out that she was so very thirsty after all. In the presence of such a rich and fresh supply, her brief worry of turning on other vampires was long forgotten.

There were two empty seats in the middle of the table. One seat was like all the others, plain and simple. The other was more or less a throne, riddled with jewels and a soft, plump cushion. When they approached the table, the masked guest closest to the throne pulled it out. Sera expected Inaka to take that seat, but to her surprise, Inaka set Sera down in it instead. Her instinct was to lunge across the table to greedily swallow everything that contained blood, but her limbs betrayed her.

While each of the other seats had a goblet and a dish in front of it, Sera's esteemed seat had nothing but an iron wrought knife. Etched into its weathered and ancient-looking leather handle were words she couldn't understand in symbols she had never seen before.

"What's this for?" Sera asked Inaka as she took a seat next to her.

"Everything we've done since we were trapped in this realm has come down to this," Inaka said. "For thousands and thousands of years, we've wanted nothing more than to return to how things once were. The strategic ending of human regimes, causing Great Wars, all of it has been an offering leading to this moment where you hold our future in your hands."

Sera made herself look at each of the other eleven guests in attendance. She realized with a start that they were all vampires, the heads of the covens.

"So you do plan to wake the gods?" Sera asked curiously. The shapeshifter had had good intel after all.

Inaka laughed again and shook her head. "Not all of them. The five of them couldn't occupy the same realm. It would only make things worse than they already are. No, we only plan to wake one." Inaka gestured to the statue on growing out of the blood symbol. Sera could see its face. The statue was carved out of obsidian and depicted a woman with long flowing hair, horns growing out from her forehead. Her eyes were closed. In one of her outstretched hands, she held a scythe, and the other held a snake. "Ours."

Sera looked from the statue to the knife in front of her to Inaka and back again. "And my role in this?"

"If you do not want to go through with this, then simply let me know." Inaka leaned forward and placed a hand over Sera's own. "But when I first saw you all those years ago, I knew that I wanted to worship you. Not everyone survives the transformation, especially not when one of us twelve changes them. You were reborn for this life, Sera. You were made to rule. And your sacrifice will give us dominion over this realm."

Sera's gaze fell on the knife again, on its obviously iron blade. "My sacrifice?"

Inaka leaned forward a little bit further. Sera was sure she was trying to reveal even more of her low-cut neckline. "You would still be you. But you would be the vessel for Mortem. You would be stronger than us all."

Sera would no longer need to seek the love of a god – she would *be* a god. She would never feel unloved again.

"Why me?" she asked. "Why now?"

Inaka nodded her head at someone just past Sera. "When I found you, we had just managed to get the last tool we needed for this sacrament." Someone from behind Sera set down a goblet in front of her, filled with blood far darker than human blood and thicker than any blood she had ever seen. Inaka tapped the hilt of the knife on the table gently. "This was the knife that killed one of Pario's angels and cut off its wings. And once we had this in our possession, the next step was to find someone worthy of being Death's vessel. And that was you, my beloved."

"That's why you changed me?" Sera asked, caught somewhere between awe and confusion.

"Even when you left me, I had hope that you would one day return." Inaka cupped Sera's cheek tenderly and smiled adoringly as she brushed a thumb over Sera's cheekbone. "The others were insistent that we find someone else, but I knew I would never want to worship anyone but you."

Sera realized then, all of a sudden, that she had an answer for the question posed to her several months ago. When is a monster not a monster?

Sera returned Inaka's gaze, a smile spreading over her face.

When you love it.

"Tell me what I need to do," Sera said, finally.

She had never seen Inaka look so proud, so full of love. Her mistress gestured to the cup in front of her. "When you're ready, you drink from the cup. And when Mortem comes for you, you give yourself to her." Inaka's hand moved to Sera's shoulder, and she squeezed gently, offering her one last comfort.

"'Therefore if anyone is for Mortem, he is a new

creation. The old has passed away. Behold, the new has come.'"

Inaka retrieved a mask identical to the one the other coven leaders had on from under her chair and pulled it over her face. They began to chant quietly, again in that language Sera couldn't recognize.

Sera closed her hand around the cup and brought it to her lips. The liquid was thick as syrup and slow moving. It tasted of wine made from white grapes and sumac and it bewildered her senses. Human blood couldn't compare to whatever this mixture was, though it made her feel as if she had just drank some poor soul dry. Power surged through her veins and she greedily drank it down, tilting her head back with a moan. When the last droplets hit her tongue and she set the cup back down on its spot, the statue of Mortem began to move. The chanting got louder as the lights all dimmed and the statue twisted and stretched.

Then an ethereal hand popped out from the statue, then the rest of her arm, then her other limbs. The obsidian she had been carved from crumbled away as she moved and freed herself from the prison she had been trapped in for several lifetimes. When she was fully formed, she stood to her full height and stretched. Mortem was massive in stature, her head grazing the roof of the cave. She took a step to crouch down in front of Sera and opened her eyes. Her irises, pupils, and sclera were all shades of red.

She reached down towards the knife on the table, and Sera found her own hand copying the movement. Gone was any trace of weariness in her bones. Instead, she felt only electric energy, only love.

The goddess picked up her own ethereal version of the knife. Sera did the same.

The goddess plunged the knife into her chest. Sera did the same.

All at once, she understood what the others around her were chanting.

"And the goddess became flesh and dwelt among us. We have seen her glory, the way to eternal life."

And Sera felt herself dying and being reborn a thousand times. Constellations exploded inside of her as she took on the power of the goddess of Death. She felt filled with glory, filled with power, filled with adoration and love.

And when she opened her eyes, she saw the world anew.

~ XIII ~

AND DEATH SHALL BE NO MORE

As the god of Death, you were worshiped and revered by many.

Most of humanity, the most populous creatures in the realm, did not notice that you had been awakened. They blamed The War on men's egos rather than on a lonely god who was experiencing true power that you had not been ready to take. When you walked among the living for too long, their hearts began to harden. Under your dark shadow, they became bitter, spiteful, jealous, and mean. They displayed a creative cruelty vampires could never possess, killing each other in new and inventive ways that seemed to delight them. They figured out how to make murder impersonal, destroying cities from opposite ends of the sea, creating machines that could trample a small town within minute. And the part of you that was more *god* than *you* took delight in it.

The vampires who worshiped you made sacrifices in your name, laying bodies you had never asked for at your feet. As more and more humans became aware of the realities of their world, that they shared it with the creatures they had once assumed to be merely fantastical, they became more and more careful. Humans kept garlic in their pockets, hung them on their door frames, planted them in their gardens. It became a game to the more depraved, trying to catch a meal and come out of it having bested a human. The game ended in death one way or another, so they began to see feeding as an act of worship. You couldn't stop them; they loved you.

There were others, though their prayers did not reach your ears unless you sought them out. The humans who worshiped you begged for a place in your kingdom. When they heard about your rebirth, they brought gifts like gold, frankincense, and myrrh as offerings, as if you had a need for such trinkets. The shapeshifters who worshiped you asked for the ability to make more of their kind by a method other than birth, as the vampires did. The fairies who worshiped you asked for nothing more than their continued longevity.

The demons did not worship you.

You felt it every time something died – from the smallest blade of grass to the most powerful vampire taken out by their own hubris. Each resonated with a very specific signature that, after a month, you were able to pinpoint. All things die.

You had your own league of angels. Magnificent things each with a mass of eyes, serene faces, impressive black wings with feathers as sharp as steel, and hardened hearts. At your command, they were visible to all in your kingdom. It was their blood that sustained you now, the delicious white wine and sumac offered to you on your throne in shining cups fit for kings and queens. Upon your return they broke away from The Organization and spent their time by your side, finding ecstasy in the presence of their god. They hosted parties that never ended, only paused whenever you had some business to attend to, some plea bargain or another to hear out. After millennia apart, the angels became intoxicated off of your nearness, dancing with dearly dedicated worshipers. You loved them, and they loved you.

Even gods have a destiny, and it is the fate of that which is created to eventually meet its end. There would come a time in the far off future when the world would cease to exist, and it was your job to be its herald.

"You will hear of wars and rumors of wars," you would tell those who gathered before you during your Mass, "but see to it that you are not alarmed. Such things must happen, but the end is still to come. Nation will rise against nation, and kingdom against kingdom. There will be famines and earthquakes in various places. All these are the beginning of birth pains."

You told them of how the world would break itself apart, eventually weighed down by the stress of carrying the realms that were never meant to be combined into one.

When you were able to get a moment alone, you would escape into your lover's arms. Your lover, who had long treated you as if you were something to be worshiped, was the only constant in your new life.

Your lover never bragged to anyone else that she alone was able to see god spread out on the shared bed, that she alone knew how god tasted from top to bottom. She knew divinity at its most vulnerable, but did not make you regret that vulnerability. Your lover's newfound purpose was to get lost in you. She never asked you for anything, never desired anything more than your attention. You let her convince you that it was all she ever wanted. You told yourself that you did not need anyone else. You loved her, and she loved you.

On slow days, you would answer for yourself all the questions you had ever had; the gods had been siblings, in a sense. You could feel them even as they slumbered beneath the ground. No matter the plans those who had served your siblings tried to make – as if you weren't omnipotent - they would never rise again. They could never rise as long as you had a physical form. You weren't sure which part of you was more proud that you had finally managed to best them; your worshipers certainly had been the most devoted. The world was completely yours.

As god, there was no one to guide you through this life as there had been when your heart first stopped beating. You were god and knew everything there was to know about the past, present, and future. Nothing surprised you, and you expected that to become boring. But you knew how things would go and how they would end, and the excitement kept you on your toes.

On occasion, the living blamed you for everything you did and didn't have a hand in. Once they learned your name, they spoke it with fear and trepidation. They preached against you as if their voracious words could ever cause you any harm. Even though most of those who professed themselves to be speaking with Pario's divinity were simply predators as you had once been (as you, technically, still were), you had love for them and those they tried to fool.

You felt love for everyone who passed through your kingdom into the afterlife you redesigned. Once you realized you had the power, you gave each and every soul the option to go to whatever afterlife they desired or to become a part of your kingdom. To dance with your angels for eternity and share in your love. Most moved on to their afterlife, but those who had been like you, those who had sorely desired love in life, stayed with you in your kingdom.

Your most loving act was to protect the one you never got to love, the one who roamed the world looking for impossible ways to bring you back. You guided her, helped her understand her newly returned magic, made monsters lurking in the dark turn a blind eye when she was near. You let yourself believe that you would be worth more to her from a distance.

You fought the old god inside your head, the one who had expected you to cover the world in blood. She offered you a kingdom of ash and bone and you rejected it in favour of one fashioned from patience and love. There were moments when you couldn't help but let it in, when the decay curled around your legs and licked its way up your chest. You learned to accept that part of you because you felt love for it as well.

In Death, there was love.

CPSIA information can be obtained
at www.ICGtesting.com
Printed in the USA
JSHW022301140622
26962JS00007B/37